UNBREAKABLE

KINGS OF RETRIBUTION MC

CRYSTAL DANIELS
SANDY ALVAREZ

SANDY ALVAREZ
CRYSTAL DANIELS

Two Pens One Story

1

JAKE

Giving up on sleep, I roll out of bed and walk over to the chair in the corner of my room, where I tossed my jeans just a few hours ago and pull them on. I don't need to look at the time to know it's too fuckin' early. I haven't slept a solid six hours since *she* left. Grace has been gone six months. Six months and one single text telling me she wasn't coming back to Polson. My gut is telling me she's runnin' from something, but what? Do I think us getting close scared her? Yes. Do I believe that is the sole reason she skipped town? No.

Something bigger is going on with Grace, and I refuse to give up until I find her, bring her home, and demand she tell me why she ran. Another thing my Little Bird will have to come to terms with is, she is mine. I know with absolute certainty, Grace wants me as much as I want her. I've given her two years of slow. Two years of letting her get used to the idea of us. If she thinks runnin' away is going to detour me, then she has another thing coming. There is one thing about me she will come to realize real soon, is that I am a very patient man. I knew from the first moment I laid eyes on Grace I was a goner. Some people may think I'm crazy or call me a pussy for waitin' around on a woman for two long ass years, but when it comes to a good woman, the *right* woman, a man will do damn near anything to make her his. Besides, I'm a forty-six-year-old man. My days of chasing meaningless pussy are over. Sure, when I was a young and dumb kid in high school, I had my fair share of meaningless fucks, and after Lily passed, I went through a rough patch where I tried to mask the pain with random club whores and bed hopping.

Once you reach a certain age in life, though, that shit becomes real old, real fast. That or you meet a woman who has you realizing you want more. When I walked into Grace's bakery, I was met with the smallest, most delicate woman. She stands at 5 feet 3 inches and has the unruliest mass of red curls I'd ever seen. Her porcelain skin was free of makeup, and I instantly became obsessed with the smattering of freckles across the bridge of her nose. When she looked at me with those crystal blue eyes of hers, I felt like I had been punched in the solar plexus.

I felt something I haven't felt since my late wife, Lily. I never thought in my wildest fuckin' dreams that I could feel for another woman what I felt for Lily. I have not been serious about another woman since her death fifteen years ago...until Grace. Within five minutes of meeting her, I sensed she had to be handled with kid gloves. Not only was she skittish around men, but I could see there was fear and pain hidden behind her eyes. I wanted to put a bullet in the head of the person who had harmed this woman.

Walking into the kitchen, I snag my keys off the hook by the front door, and I flip a couple of switches turning on my outside floodlights. At only 3:00 am, it's still dark as hell outside. I then make my way out and around to the back of my house to my shed. I live in one of the most secluded parts of Polson. Most of my brothers live near the lake, but not me. I like not having neighbors. The closest house to mine is about five miles out. I have nothin' but peace and fuckin' quiet out here. Just the way I like it. I found this place ten years ago. The old man I bought it from hadn't even finished building it. It was nothing but walls and a roof. The vision he had for the log cabin was beautiful, but his wife fell ill, and he no longer had the time to finish the home since he had to care for her. The older man was only asking for what he had already paid for out of pocket. The deal was too sweet to pass up. I spent one year fixing it up enough to make it suitable to live in before I moved in. Two years later, my home was complete.

The three-bedroom, two-bathroom cabin is my sanctuary. Unless I invite someone out here, I don't get any visitors, not counting the occasional bear or coyote. My brothers don't take offense to my isolation. I enjoy a club party or a family BBQ from time to time, but at the end of the day, when I come home, they know this place is sacred, and I don't share. When I think about sharing my home with someone, only one person comes to mind. *Grace.*

Reid has been looking for Grace for six months, but so far, he's not found shit. Grace Cohen is a ghost. Which leads us to believe that's not her real name and brings us back to my first instinct that she's runnin' from something or someone. Reid told me yesterday, he's got one more contact he has yet to use, and he is calling in a favor. I have faith my brother will come through for me. Reid is the best at what he does.

Pulling open the shed door, I flip on the lights and illuminate the 10 x 16-foot space where I keep one of my most prized possessions, a 1973 Harley Davidson XLCH Ironhead Hardtail. It belonged to my pops. He finally parted with it four years ago. It had been sitting in his garage for the better part of a decade. The stubborn older man knew he could no longer ride, and his arthritis didn't allow him to work on it either. Pops knew I loved his bike and I'd bet my left nut the son of a bitch held on to it to piss me off. I love my old man. Thinking about his ass makes me chuckle. I haven't worked on the bike as much as I'd like, but lately, with all the sleepless nights, I find myself having the time. I find keeping my hands busy calms the storm inside my head and keeps me partially sane. I had been working on cars, trucks, and bikes right alongside my pops since I was old enough to remember.

My earliest memory was of me standing on a stool bent over the hood of an old Ford with my father. My parents have been married for fifty years and together for longer and are still very much in love. My father was a mechanic, and my mother is a retired school teacher. I had your typical upbringing and was an only child. My parents struggled for five years to get pregnant with me, and my mother went through a complicated delivery that left her unable to bear any more children. They both still live in the same house I grew up in and are still very independent. I call every day and go by their place at least three or four times a week to visit them.

I inherited my love of mechanics from my pops. Kings Custom wasn't always Kings Custom. My pops was the original owner. Back when he started the garage, it was called Delane's. I always knew I would one day take over the garage. College wasn't for me. That's why the day after I graduated high school, my lifelong friend Bennett and I enlisted in the Army.

Joining the service was something I had been contemplating for a couple of years, and though my parents were nervous about the what-ifs, they were also proud and supportive. Serving my country was something I felt was my calling. I don't think Bennett felt the same as me, but he told me he wasn't going to let me go off to war and not have my back. The two of us grew up together, so it only seemed natural we enlist together. We both served eight years before deciding it was time to move on. We'd seen enough. When our service was over, Bennett and I tried falling back into some sort of routine. Pops had both of us working in the garage, and for the most part, we were adjusting back into civilian life well, but something was missing, we both felt it. It was about one year after being home when things changed. I received a call from Sean, a buddy of mine I served with. He and a couple of his friends were passing through Montana and asked if Bennett and I would like to catch up. The next day Sean and his friends rolled into town on their bikes.

Throughout the weekend, I learned one of the guys grew up around an MC. He told us about how they were a group of veterans, and forming the club was a way for them to get back what they missed the most...camaraderie. It was right then, and there The Kings were born, and I became their President. Bennett was a medic in the Army, and though he enjoyed working in the garage with me, it's not where his heart was. So, he and his wife, Lisa, started doing community service. Lisa runs a soup kitchen in town and Bennett spends most days offering his medical assistance to the homeless. No, he is not an actual doctor, but he can give necessary medical attention to those less fortunate. He even has a few resources at the local hospital that aid in providing the supplies he needs. These are the things that most of the people in our community don't see. People see what they want. They see a biker gang.

It pisses me off when people assume MCs are only about breaking the law and not following the rules, but that's not the truth. Not for The Kings anyway.

Do we always follow the law? No. Do we live by our own set of rules? Hell, fuckin' yeah. We break the law, and we've even done shit I'm not proud of. There have been times when the club has steered onto the wrong path because we became obsessed with the cash flow it provided, but after reaping the consequences of our past choices, I have done everything in my power to give the club a new direction. Regardless, each one of my men is honorable and would give a stranger the shirt off our back and would also lay down our lives for those we love; me included. I won't lie and say I haven't taken a life because I have. More than I can count—both in and out of the service. I will tell you this, though; I have not put a bullet in someone unless they have deserved it. I have no qualms about ridding this earth of scum. I am fully prepared to meet my maker when my time is up and answer for my sins.

Walking into the shed, I sit down on the stool next to the bike. I can't fuckin' wait until she's runnin'. Whenever I look at it, all I imagine is me cruisin' down the road with Grace on the back and her arms wrapped around my waist. I've only had one other woman on the back of my bike, and that's Lily. I met Lily six months after coming home from the Army. I remember the day like it was yesterday. I was working in the garage, and it was pouring fucking rain outside and in walks the most beautiful woman I had ever seen. Lily was soaked from head to toe. Her car had broken down about a mile down the road. She was 5 feet 8 inches tall, curves for days, with long brown hair and eyes the color of honey. Lucky for her, we were the only garage in town open on a Saturday. After that day, I guess all I can say is the rest was history. Lily and I became inseparable. We fell in love and married a few short months after the day she walked into my life.

She was there by my side when I started the club. We hardly had any money. Every penny I had saved went into buying the building that is currently our clubhouse. We didn't have a place of our own, but we made the clubhouse our home. Not once did Lily complain. She said all she wanted was to be with me. As long as we were together, then that was enough for her. Two years after the club was started, the garage got its first custom bike job. One satisfied customer later, and we began receiving more and more custom requests.

When Pops saw the kind of success the garage was having, he handed over the keys, and that is when Kings Custom was born. A few months later our lives took a turn when Lily received a devastating call, and I was by her side when she was told her sister

Rose had died in a car accident. There was no question about the decision to take Logan in and raise him. I had become close to Lily's nephew and was fond of her sister. My wife had confided in me one day and told me the story of Rose and Logan's father.

Then three and a half years after we were married, I was by her side when she was diagnosed with cervical cancer. I never in my dreams thought someone so young would have to face something like that. I spent four of the best years of my life with Lily before she succumbed to cancer. The whole ordeal was swift and unexpected, but I was at her side until the very end. In Lily's final days, she made me promise a few things: take care of her nephew, Logan, and raise him to be the best man he can be. Two: find someone to share my life with. Number one was a no-brainer. I loved Logan as if he were my son and would be honored to raise him, but her last promise I couldn't. How was I going to be able to move on? I loved Lily with everything I had. She was it for me. I would never find another woman that could make me feel the way Lily did, so I thought.

When a person loses a spouse, moving on can feel like a tug-of-war. One day you meet someone and boom, that person suddenly sparks something inside you, something you haven't felt in a long time. And when you recognize what's happening, there is a tiny shred of guilt that creeps in. For me, even though my wife is gone, a small part of me felt as though I was replacing her. I was letting another woman into my heart and making me feel in a way that only Lily had. Then one day, I realized, Grace is not a better woman than Lily was, just different.

Were my feelings for Grace going to take away the feelings I had and continue to have for my late wife? No. I think back to the words Lily spoke to me before she died. *"Don't waste a moment of your precious life or the love you have to give. Find someone to share it with, and when you find the right woman, I want you to hold onto her with everything you have and know that you have my blessing. I want*

CRYSTAL DANIELS & SANDY ALVAREZ

you to be happy, Jake." I knew the minute I decided Grace was going to mine, and I was going to stop at nothing till she was, that Lily had already given me her blessing years ago. I had fulfilled my first promise of raising Logan, and as soon as I find my woman, I would fulfill my second.

A smile tugs at my lips when I think back to last night. The club had a party in the clubhouse to celebrate the adoption of Breanna. I am damn proud of the man Logan has become. I want to take credit and say it was all me, but it wasn't. His woman, Bella, had a lot to do with the man he is today. I know his mom and his aunt would be proud of him too. Besides my club, Logan is my greatest accomplishment. He doesn't have my blood runnin' through his veins, but he is my son. I always hoped for children of my own, but as I got older, I no longer longed for it. I consider Gabriel, Reid, Quinn, Logan, and all the young men in my club to be my sons. I have a history with every one of them. I love all of them as if they were mine and I would give my life for my boys. God may not have blessed me with my own children, but he has blessed me with my boys, my brothers...my club. To those men, I am their father, their brother, and I am their President.

Looking up from the bike, I can see the sun is beginning to rise over the mountains, and when I look down at my watch, it reads 6:00 am. Tossing my wrench back in the toolbox to my left, I stand and pull a rag from my back pocket to wipe the grease from my calloused hands. Striding out of the shed, I pull the double doors closed and secure in place the padlock. I hear the ping of my cell phone alerting me to a text. Removing it from my front pocket, I open a message from Reid.

Reid: *Logan and I are waiting for you at the clubhouse.*
Me: *On my way.*
I'm hoping he has some news on where my woman is.

2

GRACE

Swiping beads of sweat from my brow with the back of my hand, I continue to wipe the tables clean. I lean over and retrieve the three-dollar tip the customer left folded underneath the salt shaker and place it inside my apron pocket. The only place I could find work in this tiny town here in North Dakota was a truck stop diner about ten miles from the Canadian border. Today I'm wrapping up a double shift. Tracie, a young mother of two, called in just as I was about to clock out at lunch because her little boys were sick. Needing the extra cash, I volunteered to cover her shift for the evening.

Janet, my boss, walks around the counter and starts to help by refilling the salt shakers. "I really appreciate you staying tonight, Grace," she says with an exhausted breath.

"You're welcome, Janet. Truth be told, I could use the extra money," I admit.

"Sorry, I can't offer you more hours regularly, hon. I wish I could, but ever since the plant down the road shut down, we've lost all the business it brought in," she tells me with worry in her voice.

I'd been in town for a little over a week before I decided to stay awhile. At least long enough to save some more money and decide what my next move was going to be. Anyway, Janet's diner was the last place in town I hadn't been to. She isn't wrong in saying she can't afford much. On an average day, we possibly get a few dozen patrons at best come through here for something to eat. Most of her customers are truckers passing through to Canada. I'm guessing she took pity on me the day I walked in asking for a job. Once she let me down as sweet as possible that she wasn't hiring, I sat at a table picking at a sandwich for the better part of two hours trying to strategize what town I would travel to next. Before getting up to leave, Janet had stopped me and offered me a job after all. I started the very next day. "I'm more than grateful for the hours I do have, Janet. No need to apologize." I toss my cleaning cloth onto the counter and start removing my apron.

"You ready?" she asks her keys jingling in her hand as she flings her bag over her shoulder.

My car gave out this morning on my way to work. Just sputtered out and died. I'm sure ignoring the check engine light for over a month might have had something to do with it. My extent of mechanical knowledge ends after checking the oil and changing a tire. But, getting it repaired will have to wait until I've saved up a few more paychecks. Until then, Janet has offered to give me a ride home, and Ben, the cook, offered to tow it to the local garage for me over the weekend. "More than ready," I yawn.

Stepping outside, I wait for Janet to lock the door before we get into her old rusty truck. It's a standard. Something I've heard everyone should learn how to drive, but I never did. Growing up in a city environment, we commuted either by foot, train, or bus. "I appreciate the ride, Janet. Hopefully, in the next couple of weeks, I can get my car looked at. I hope it's a minor repair," I express to her. My phone vibrates in the front pocket of my jeans. Pulling it out, I swipe my finger across the screen to read the text message and smile.

"If you don't mind coming in an hour earlier, I can pick you up in the morning, and I'm sure we can find you a ride once your shift ends tomorrow," she offers as she rolls her truck to stop at the only traffic light in town.

"I don't mind at all," I tell her. Reaching into my purse, I find my keys as Janet pulls into the small parking space in front of the duplex I share with the guy next door.

"Alright, hon. I'll see you in the morning. Take care and get some rest." She smiles warmly.

Opening the truck door, I slide out. "Goodnight, Janet, and thanks again," I tell her. After closing the door, I look over my shoulder, giving her a smile and a small wave as I unlock my door. She waits for me to walk inside before I hear her tires crunch the gravel and pull away.

Dog tired, I kick my shoes off at the door, letting them land wherever and toss my purse on the table sitting near the front window. Eager to soak in a warm bath, I wander down the hall peeling my clothes off along the way. Flipping the dim light on over the bathroom sink, I drop my shirt into the hamper. After turning the water on, I let the tub start to fill before adding some honey milk bubble bath. It's the one splurge I allow for myself. Reaching behind my back, I unclasp my bra and let out a satisfied sigh. I swear freeing the girls at the end of the day has to be one of the best feelings in the world. Once I've peeled my jeans down my legs, I discard them with the rest of my clothes and throw them in the hamper and step into the tub. The instant I submerge myself in the warm water and take in the scent of honey, my tired muscles relax. I allow myself for a few minutes to drift off. Not asleep, I meditate. Clear my mind. I was taught to do this a long time ago. Finding my center and meditation has helped me overcome many mental obstacles. It's helped me to focus.

The stillness I'm sated in is abruptly broken with a knock on the front door. Assuming it's my neighbor, who has made it clear on more than one occasion he likes me, I ignore it. Not that he isn't a good-looking guy. He's not *him*. Another knock on the door causes me to sigh, and I abandoned my attempts to enjoy the rest of my night in the tub.

Climbing out, I quickly dry, and throw my robe on, and tie the sash snuggly around my waist. Before I make it down the short hallway, he knocks again, this time a little harder than the time before. Irritation sets in, and usually, I'm not confrontational. I keep to myself, but I've just done a double shift. I've been on my feet all day, and I've had my fair share of men for the day. I let all this make me momentarily forget that I should never open the door without looking out the window first or make the person on the other side announce who they are. Without thinking, I swing the front door open. I'm shocked to see the person staring back at me. *Detective Finn O'Rourke.* "Why are you here?"

With one hand on the door frame and the other at his side, he stands, filling my front doorway. His eyes trained on mine, he opens his mouth, "Anna, what are you doing?"

What am I doing? Why the hell would he ask me what I'm doing? I'm doing the same damn thing I've been doing for two years. Hiding. Surviving. I glare at him and cross my arms under my breasts. "Don't call me Anna." I stare him down, hard, and do my best to be intimidating. By the small smirk appearing on his face, I'm not doing a very good job of convincing him not to mess with me. Why would it? I'm the size of a toddler compared to Finn.

"First," he stands at his full height, getting ready to give me a speech, "you opened this fucking door without checking to see who was standing on the other side and two-you've been MIA for the better part of a month. I'm worried about you. Now, are you going to make my ass stand out here all night?" he chastises.

I knew he would show up eventually. I step aside, clearing a

I hate when I feel weak. People are relying on me to keep my shit together. I close my eyes and even my breathing.

"Good. Focus. Draw your strength from within you. It's there. Draw from those who matter most to you, Grace," Finn says before pulling back and looking at me, "I promise. I will get him," he affirms, then kisses my forehead.

Finn is a good man. One of the best I've ever come across. He is the protective brother I never had. I don't know the exact number of women he has helped over the years—that number is irrelevant. What I do feel is he genuinely cares about everyone. I believe he sees his sister in the face of all of us. He has helped keep me alive and find a new beginning. His sister's case was a violent and tragic one, which is his story to tell, but he does all this for her and for himself, and I know we will forever be indebted to him. Finn will always be a part of my life, even after the mess I'm in straightens itself out. "It's getting late. Why don't you sleep before you disappear on me," I offer. I know how far he came to get here, and I know he drove.

"Use of your couch and something to eat would be great, but I need to head out early. I don't want anyone to see me leaving here," he says to me as I get off the couch and walk to the refrigerator.

"I've got some leftover meatloaf in here. I can make us a sandwich?" I look at him.

"That would be great," he answers.

Surprisingly, he doesn't push the issue on Jake or Polson as we sit and eat our meal, which I'm grateful for.

"I met with Glory earlier today. Everything is good," he reaches into his front pocket and pulls out a cell phone and hands it to me, "I gave her a new one too. Give them a call on it and give me the other one so I can dispose of it." He keeps his hand open, waiting.

I walk over toward the front door and grab my phone from the inside of my purse and bring it to him, placing it on his open palm, "I'm going to walk back to my room and give them a call. I won't be but a minute. I'll bring you a blanket and pillow when I come back," I inform him and walk away.

After making the call, I retrieve a blanket from the linen closet and grab one of the two pillows off my bed. When I walk back into the small living room, Finn is lightly snoring on the couch. He looks ridiculous, scrunched up on the little piece of furniture. Finn is around six feet with reddish-brown hair and gray eyes. He's fit. Not overly muscular, just enough, you can tell it no matter what clothes he wears. From what I know about him, he grew up in the ring. His father was a boxer, as was his grandfather before. Instead of making a career of it, he went into law enforcement.

Unfolding the blanket, I drape it across him and place the pillows on the back of the couch for him to use later. Securing the locks on the front door, I turn off all the lights leaving the one over the stove on. Because I have Finn sleeping in the next room, I feel an extra sense of security, and it doesn't take long for me to fall asleep.

———

WHEN I WAKE the next morning, Finn is sitting on the couch with his elbows on his knees with a coffee mug in his hand. It's early, and the sun hasn't begun to rise yet. I knew he would leave before daybreak, which is why I set my alarm to get out of bed a couple of hours earlier than normal.

"Just made the coffee. Left some for you," he gestures, lifting his cup toward the kitchen.

Shuffling my tired feet across the floor, I pour a cup for myself and sit down beside him.

"I want you to go back," he tells me.

"I can't," I reply, warming my hands with the heat of the mug.

"I'm heading that way. I need to make sure you didn't leave

anything behind. Just in case you don't listen to me." Finn sits his cup down on the table and starts slipping on his shoes.

"I made sure nothing was left, and I'm not going back." I roll my neck, trying to work the kinks out.

Knowing I've dug my heels in, Finn lets out a heavy sigh, places his hands on his lap, and pushes off the couch. He puts his phone and wallet in his pockets.

"I know it's hard, Grace, but I'm asking you to trust your heart this time. Not every man is Ronan. I think you already see that in Jake. Trust in it." He slips his suit jacket on, then grabs my shoulder and pulls me in for a hug.

I don't know how to respond. I squeeze him back.

"I'll be in touch. Please think about what I've said," Finn urges.

Nodding, I walk him to the door. Stepping out, he waits for me to close and lock it. Peering out my window halfway down the driveway, he turns and gives me a short wave. He didn't park here, but somewhere nearby. It's his way of making sure he isn't followed. I watch him walk down the street until he disappears amongst the shadows of the predawn darkness. I have four hours before I have to be at work, so I make my way to my room and climb back into bed. I lay there wishing things could be different, and when I close my eyes, I dream of a better life; in Polson.

3

JAKE

I'm driving down Main Street on my way to the clubhouse when I pass Grace's bakery. My gut clenches when I cut my eyes over and see the lights off and the closed sign on the front door. The Cookie Jar has been my first stop of the day for the past two years. The only time I have ever seen Grace close the bakery is one weekend out of every month. In two years, those weekends are the only times I have not put eyes on her. The past six months have been killing me. I'm hoping Reid has some news for me this morning on where she may be, or hell, anything would be nice. Something that would give us a clue as to why she's using a fake name and what brought her to Polson.

Pulling up to the clubhouse, I see Logan and Reid's bikes, and I park next to them. When I stride inside, my nostrils are assaulted with the smell of stale beer, cigarettes, and the place is a fuckin' mess. Peering to my right, I see Liz passed out on top of Sean. It looks like things got a little wild last night after I left. The door slamming shut behind me startles them awake. "Get this shit cleaned up," I bark at her.

Usually, a prospect would be on top of this shit, but since we currently only have one, she gets the pleasure of cleaning up. The fact that I can't stand the bitch might have a little bit to do with it as well. I used to be able to tolerate Liz, but after the shit show with her and Cassie a couple of years ago, I have a bad taste in my mouth when it comes to her. It's only because of Sean, and a few of the other guy's votes are what's keeping her ass here. I'm waiting for her to slip up and give me cause to kick her to the curb. The whore's time is limited, mark my word. Liz has this conniving look in her eyes, and I don't trust one hair on her head. Oh, she thinks she has some of us brothers fooled, and she thinks her pussy is fuckin' gold. The bitch is sorely mistaken. Plus, she's not been pulling her weight around here. Our new girls Raine and Ember, have been some of the best club girls we've had in years. They take care of the brothers, respect the old ladies, and never complain. When Liz gets up off the sofa, she does so with a huff. "You got a fuckin' problem? Because if your ass doesn't like my orders, you know where the door is," I say staring her down and my tone daring the bitch to say something back.

Thinning her lips and looking down at the floor, I watch as she scurries past me doing what she's told. *Smart move.*

"What's up your ass this mornin', Prez?" Sean pipes up from his perch on the sofa.

He looks like death warmed over. The man is my age but acts like a fuckin' fifteen-year-old. He's never been married or even been close to settling down in his life. The man is completely satisfied with sticking his dick in one club whore after another.

Turning my glare toward him, "What's up my ass is walking in here, and I'm rewarded with a goddamn mess that stinks of garbage and piss. You all are a bunch of grown-ass men. If you want to party and have a good time, then be my guest, but for Christ's sake, clean up after yourselves. You got me?"

Lifting his brow and holding up his hands in defense, Sean

knows better than to challenge my sour mood. "Yeah, Prez, I got ya."

Satisfied with his response, I turn on my heel and make my way down the hall to my office. On the way there, I pass Quinn who is sitting at the bar. The dipshit is smirking but smart enough to keep his hole shut. Hell, I know I'm overreacting this morning. This isn't the first time I've walked into the club being a pigsty after a party, and it won't be the last. It's just my nerves are on edge, and it's best everyone around me tread lightly.

No sooner does my ass hit the chair behind my desk when Reid and Logan come striding in. "Prez," they both acknowledge with a nod before taking a seat in front of me. "You got anything for me this mornin'?" I ask, looking at Reid.

With a grim expression, he shakes his head. "Sorry, Prez. We still can't find shit. Whoever Grace had helped her disappear did a damn good job."

Taking my ball cap off my head, I toss it on my desk and run my palm down my tired face and through my beard. *Fuck.*

"I know we've already been through Grace's apartment, but maybe we should go back and take another look around. See if she left anything behind. Something we may have missed that would give us a clue," Logan chimes in.

"Yeah, maybe you're right. Can't hurt to take another look around. You two feel like ridin' over there with me? Quinn and Austin can cover the garage today."

"You got it, Prez," they both say, standing from their seats, and the three of us walk back through the clubhouse and out to our bikes.

After parking our bikes in front of the bakery, I walk around to the side of the building and make my way up the stairs that lead to Grace's apartment with Logan and Reid trailing behind. After we discovered Grace had left, I had Reid change the locks on the door since I did not have a key, and I wanted to be able to gain access any time I wanted. Fishing the key out of my pocket, I unlock the door, and the three of us walk inside. We don't make it but a few steps in the apartment when a man rounds the corner of the bathroom with his gun drawn and pointed straight at me. It only takes my brothers and me three point two seconds to pull our pieces.

The four of us engage in an intense stare off for several seconds before I see something flash over the motherfucker's face. Something almost like recognition, and even though he keeps his weapon trained on me, I notice his shoulders lose some of its tension.

"You mind telling me who the fuck you are and why the hell you're in this apartment?" I square off. Not looking the least bit intimidated at three bikers pointing their guns at him, the man answers my question.

"I'm Detective Finn O'Rourke. And I could ask you the same thing Jake Delane, but I already know the answer to that question."

At the mention of my name coming out of his mouth, my nostrils flare, and I grit my teeth. Why the fuck would a detective be in Grace's apartment, and why would he make it his business to know who I am...unless he's investigation something that has to do with Grace, and like every other pig, they assume the local MC is responsible.

"You can wipe that look off your face, Mr. Delane. I'm not here for you or your club," he says, lowering his weapon and placing it back in its holster. "I've put my weapon away, and I would appreciate it if you, Mr. Kane, and Mr. Carter, would do the same. As I said, I'm not here for you."

Knowing my brothers won't take orders from anyone in this room except me, I look over my shoulder and give Logan and Reid the signal to put their piece away. Afterward, I turn my attention back to the detective. "If you're not here for my club or me, you mind telling me why you are here and in Grace's apartment?"

Walking over to the small kitchenette, O'Rourke casually leans against the counter and crosses his arms over his chest. I take a moment to size him up. The man is about 6 feet tall, with reddish-brown hair, and in decent shape. Every move he makes is skillful and with purpose. I'd say he's some sort of fighter or trainer. He looks almost relaxed, but I can tell by his body language he's acutely aware of his surroundings and is ready for anything. After a moment, O'Rourke finally speaks. "Let me ask you, Mr. Delane, who is Grace to you?"

Standing taller and without hesitation, I answer his question, "Grace is mine."

I'd be lying if I said the smile that just came across the detective's face didn't confuse me. What the hell is he playing at?

"I thought as much," he says.

"Are we going to quit with all this cryptic bullshit and get down to some fuckin' answers," Logan pipes in from behind me.

"Fair enough," O'Rourke says, blowing out a breath. "Grace is a friend of mine. She is someone I have been helping the past few years, and she also is someone I care about very much." At the growl that escapes me, O'Rourke is quick to stress his words. "Grace is strictly a friend. She's more like a sister, I assure you." Studying the sincerity of his words for a moment, I gesture for him to continue while I fight to reign in my temper. "Anyway, I will not give you the details of mine and Grace's relationship because I feel that is her story to tell. What I can tell you is Grace moving to Polson was my doing. I chose this town on purpose and one of those purposes being your club. Grace had some shit happen to her, and she needed a place to lay low and a place where I felt she would be protected. I know about your club Mr. Delane, and though you and The Kings are sometimes into some shady shit, I also know that you all go to great lengths to protect your community. Nothing goes on in Polson without you knowing about it, and there are not too many people who would go head to head with The Kings."

"So, let me get this straight," Reid steps forward and interjects. "Grace, whom we already know is not likely her real name, and I am going to assume you're doing this because she was in danger and needed a place to hide. You set her up in Polson and based on the club's reputation, you felt like here was the safest place for her?"

"Yes," O'Rourke answers. "My gut told me without a doubt; she would be safe in Polson. And my gut has never steered me wrong."

Fuck. I'm finding it hard not to like the son of a bitch. I stay silent for a minute as I let his words sink in. Then I ask my next question. "You know where Grace is, don't ya?"

Nodding his head, O'Rourke answers, "Yeah, I know where she is, and I'm sorry, but I can't tell you. Grace doesn't trust easily, and I won't do anything to break the trust she has in me. What I can tell you is she's safe, and I am doing everything I can to convince her to come back. I still believe Polson is the safest place for her. I am doing everything within my power to eliminate the threat against her, but that shit is not going well. I need more time. She has insisted she won't be returning to Polson. I came back here today to make sure she didn't leave anything. She said she was in a hurry to leave but did do a proper sweep of the place. She knows not to leave any evidence behind. I came anyway just to be sure. I'm assuming that's what you all were coming here for. I'm sorry to say you wouldn't have found anything. I have taught her well. She is very good at covering her tracks."

"Did whoever is after Grace find her? Is that why she left?" I ask.

"No. Grace got spooked, and that is why she left. I think you already know that though, don't you, Mr. Delane?"

I don't answer because it was more of a statement than a

question. Shoving off from his perch on the counter, the detective makes his way to the door. "Grace is a very strong-willed woman, and one thing I've come to learn about her over the years is she sometimes needs a little push."

When he opens the door, he pauses and regards us one last time.

"You know, I just came from this little place called J's Diner in North Dakota. They make the best pancakes I've ever had. You should check it out sometime." With those parting words, O'Rourke walks out of the apartment.

"I'll be damned," Logan hisses. "Did that motherfucker just tell you where your woman is?"

At Logan's question, I cut my eyes to Reid, and I don't have to say a word.

"On it, Prez."

Roughly an hour later, we are back at the clubhouse, and Reid has all I need to know. Now I am holding an emergency church. Slamming the gavel down, I have the floor and my brothers' attention. "I called this meeting because I am going to be out of town. I leave first thing in the mornin', and I don't know how long I'll be gone. A couple of days at best. Logan will be in charge while I'm away. If any of you has shit that needs handling, you bring it to him. Are there any questions?" I peer around the table at all my men, letting my gaze stop when it lands on Quinn and his raised hand. *Fuckin' Quinn.* Blowing out an exasperated breath and narrowing my hard eyes at the dip shit in question, I ask, "What is it, man? And if you plan on letting something smart come out of your mouth, then think twice before you do because I'll put a bullet in your ass and you won't be able to sit down for a month."

"Damn Prez, no need to get all snippy. I was going to ask where you were going."

"I'm going to get my woman and bring her home," I announce.

And with those words, I slam the gavel down, with a chorus of "hell yeah" filling the room.

"If you run into any trouble and need back up, you give us a call Prez. We'll have your back." This is coming from Gabriel, and I acknowledge him with a chin lift.

"Appreciate it, brother." I bring my attention to Quinn.

"My pops needs some yard work done out at his place tomorrow, Quinn. You get the pleasure of taking care of that chore for me," I say with a smirk.

"Oh, come on now, Prez. You know your dad hates me. He's always ridin' my ass and giving me a hard time. Can't one of the other brothers go?" he whines like a five-year-old.

He's not wrong, my pops loves fucking with Quinn, but what my brother doesn't know is my father is rather fond of him, he likes fuckin' with him.

"Damn," Quinn grumbles. "Your mom better have something good to eat. Her cookin' alone is worth putting up with your old man."

I shake my head and chuckle. Quinn, in many ways, is still the same little kid who followed Logan and Reid home from school one day. Word is they fended off a bully for him, and they were never able to shake him since. I'll always remember the gleam I saw in the kid's eyes the first time he hung around the clubhouse. It was the same look I've seen in the eyes of every one of my brothers—the look of belonging. Shaking myself from the past, I take one final look around the table at the men I call my family. I give them all one last nod before walking out the door and toward my future.

5:00 am the next morning, and I've already been on the road for an hour. After church yesterday, I immediately came home to pack and hopefully get a few hours of sleep before making the ten-hour drive to Crosby, North Dakota. It took Reid all of five minutes yesterday to pin down Grace's location after O'Rourke in a roundabout way ratted her out. He also found out that Detective O'Rourke is from Chicago. He's lived there his whole life. It also leads me to believe that is where Grace is from, or at least where she was living before moving to Polson. So now, Reid is using that little bit of information to see what else he can dig up on Grace and her past. I respect the man because he has a sense of loyalty to Grace and because he wants to keep her safe, but I could also tell he wanted her back in Polson. He was right when he said it was the best place for her. There is no safer place for her than with me. And she will be with me, in my house and my bed. I dare any motherfucker who comes into my town and thinks they can harm my Little Bird. Just thinking about the shit show at hand has me gripping the handlebars of my bike so hard my knuckles turn white. So, my first step is to go and claim my woman. Once we are back home and I've shown Grace what it is to be mine, I then will stop at nothing to find the bastard who is after her and, once I do, I will enjoy every second of torture he has coming his way before I end his life with a bullet between his eyes.

4

GRACE

I keep playing Finn's words over and over again in my head. To the point, it's made it hard to focus. Not even meditation has helped. It's nagging at me. With all my heart, I want to go back to Polson. I want so much for the town and the people in it to become our permanent little slice of heaven. But, my head is telling me no. Why risk it. Staying in one place for too long has messed with my thinking. Disrupted what I think is best to stay one step or more in front of my husband.

Then there's Jake. President of the local motorcycle club— The Kings of Retribution. Jake is a large man. Not only in size but in presence. At six feet three inches, he fills any space he's in. He carries himself in a way that demands attention without speaking a single word. It's captivating. Jake is in his forties, but looking at his body, you wouldn't think it. Staying physically fit is important to him. I think it stems from his years in the military. His short dark hair has a bit of gray dusting right at his temples and tapers toward the back, and his striking blue eyes pierce my soul whenever he looks at me. I knew better. Everything about him should have told me to steer clear of him, but instead, everything about him appealed to all my senses. I put up a fight —tried to reinforce the wall I placed between us. Somehow, he always found a way to slip past all my defenses. He looked at me like he knew, like he saw the real me underneath. *He could see Anna.*

I'm quiet and soft-spoken. I've never been the type to draw attention to myself. I don't wear flashy clothes or makeup, I'm understated, and that's alright with me, which is why I couldn't understand what Jake saw in me. A plain Jane, tiny redhead with way too many freckles.

When Finn told me about his plan for setting me up in Polson, I wasn't too sure. It was further away from Buffalo, South Dakota than I wanted to be. It meant longer drives and possibly less often. That alone made me sick to my stomach. Finn assured me that this move might end up being my last, and he was so confident in his statement, he even paid the rent for a whole year on a building that was set up with everything I would need to open a bakery of my own. It meant I could start truly building a future. Even hope to settle down for good. I let myself think it was possible. For a couple of years, as hard as it was, I made it all work.

That being said, I don't trust men. I wanted to believe Jake. He isn't a bad guy. Maybe in the eyes of the law, he may have done some bad things, but I don't see that when I look at him. I know everything he does is to protect the ones he loves and cares for. The thing is I trusted my heart once before, and it betrayed me. I let it blindly lead me in the direction of heartache and fear. Loving a man again put me at risk. I won't allow that to happen again, no matter how much I want to.

I open my eyes. Turning my head, I stare into the flicker of the candle sitting on the corner edge of the bathtub. Today was another long day on my feet. I did, however, finally get the opportunity to get back in the kitchen before opening this morning and baked a few things. Janet loved them so much she set them out for the customers and gave me half the earnings in sales. It felt good to be in the kitchen doing what I love.

I've been baking since I was little. My mom owned a bakery called The Sugar Shop in Chicago. Her mother and father owned the business, then passed it down to her. My grandparents were Irish immigrants. My parents were born here in the United States as was I. They made a good life for themselves. I grew up in a strong family and knew what I wanted to be when I grew up. Just like my mom and my nana before her. Strong, hard-working women. My father died when I was twenty after being mugged and attacked one-night walking home from the general store down the road from where we lived. One of the officers showed up on our doorstep that night to tell my mother and me what had happened. Not having our own transportation, he drove us to the hospital in his patrol car. Daddy held on long enough to see the loves of his life because he never made it through surgery. A few months before we lost my dad, I met Ronan. At the time, I still lived with my parents. I can't say it was love at first sight. Truth be told, he was far different than the guys I was attracted to. A bit on the shorter side but still much taller than myself. He wasn't unfit. I would say he had a runner's body, very slim and toned. His hair a dark shade of brown and brown eyes.

Before I knew it, one meeting with Ronan De Burca led to another. I fell head over heels in love with him. My mom and dad, however, didn't like him so much. You see, Ronan's family is well known. Depending on who you talk to, his family members are good pillars of the community, and to others, they say there is more than meets the eye. My parents told me time and time again that no good has come from their bloodline. They said the De Burca family built their wealth and empire on the backs and from the blood of others. When I look back, they were right. They were all right.

The fact I didn't heed my family and friends warnings eats at me every day. He doted on me, always showed up with flowers in his hand, and paid for every date. He took me out and introduced me to his parents as the love of his life. I had stars in my eyes when I looked at Ronan.

I wanted to make him happy. I placed his happiness above my own. If he didn't like my hair down, I would wear it up. If he didn't like the dress I wore, I changed it. All to please him. I didn't recognize it as control at the time until it was too late. We got married a year later, a few months after I turned twenty-one. I wanted my mom to be the one to give me away, but she wasn't supportive of my choice to marry a man she didn't approve of. It broke my heart. I wanted her to love and accept him, but I didn't let her opinion of him affect mine. Ronan would always assure me my mom was only having a hard time letting go of her only child. So, I believed him. Believing in him—in us was the worst mistake I have ever made in my life, and I've been spending the last two years running from him to save ours.

SHIT. I overslept. Blinking again, I rub my eyes to make sure I read the clock on my phone right. I should have been at the diner almost an hour ago. I look over at the alarm clock sitting on my nightstand to find it flashing. *Dammit.* The storm that rolled through last night must have knocked the power out momentarily while I was asleep. I throw the blanket off and jump out of bed. Rushing, I toss some clothes on and undo the braid from my hair, which is the only way with all these curls I won't wake up to a matted mess. Snatching my car keys from the kitchen counter, I grab my things and head to the door. Yesterday while at work, the guy from the mechanic shop came by. It turns out my battery cables came loose and needed replacing. He said it was a simple fix, and the check engine light was on due to an

O2 sensor, which he also replaced. Lucky for me I had enough to pay him for his time. Thanks to Finn. After I told him about my car, he took some money from his wallet and insisted I use it to make sure my car got fixed. He's done so much for me. I don't know how I can ever repay him and it's not enough to say thank you.

Parking my car behind the diner next to Janet's truck, I rush inside. The place is busy with our usual morning rush. Slipping my apron over my head, I tie the sash and step behind the counter where Janet has her hands full. "I'm so sorry I'm late," I express.

"That's okay, hon. It happens to us all. Could you take these orders to table 6 and 8 for me?" she asks while balancing a few plates in her hands, "Oh, and table 2 needs a coffee," she shouts over her shoulder walking off.

I grab the plates and take them to the hungry waiting customers. After making sure their orders are to their liking, I leave them to enjoy their meals. As I'm walking past tables to grab a fresh pot of coffee to take to table two, I hear *his* deep voice.

"Good morning, Little Bird."

My steps falter, and I have to catch myself by grabbing the edge of the table beside me and close my eyes. My heart thuds against my ribcage. My body reacts the same as it did before. Warmth engulfs my hand, and lighting bolts dance across my skin when a hand takes hold of mine—*his hand*. I prepare myself to see anger for leaving the way I did. He deserves so much more than me. So much more than the lies and secrets I've had to hide. Lifting my head, my eyes connect with his. His piercing blue eyes don't show any sign of hate or anger. They show worry, longing, and dare I say, love. "Jake," I whisper his name.

His eyes close. Like he's soaking me in. His thumb starts to stroke the fast beating pulse on my wrist. "I always knew you were waiting to fly away, but I have to admit I wasn't ready. My heart wasn't ready, Grace."

His words cause a major crack in my already crumbling exterior.

"How long are you working today, beautiful?" Jake asks with his eyes still fixed on me, and his hand still covering mine.

I lick my lips, "My shift ends at two," I offer.

Jake stands, taking his wallet from his back pocket and slips a ten underneath his empty cup of coffee. His body fills the space between us. I breathe him in. He always smells like cedar, mixed with the leather of his cut.

Brushing my hair aside, he bends and whispers in his husky gravely tone, "I'll be waiting for you outside at two o'clock, Little Bird," he promises. My skin comes alive with goosebumps from his warm breath against my neck.

"Okay," I answer him timidly.

I don't turn to watch him walk out the door. I only listen for the sound of the bell jingling and then the rumble of his Harley as he fires it up and leaves. I stay frozen in my spot, tuning the noise out, until I feel a light touch on my shoulder.

"Honey, you okay?" Janet questions, and I shake off the remaining effect Jake had on me.

"Um, yeah, I'm fine," I try to convince her, but the look on her face says otherwise.

"Mmhmm. Honey, the moment that man touched you, the temperature in this building went up eighty degrees. Oh, what I'd give to have a man look at me like that again," Janet remarks as she fans herself with one of the menus.

"He's just an old friend passing through. That's all," I tell her, walking behind the counter to finish my previous task and grab the pot of coffee from the hot plate.

"You keep on telling yourself that, dear," Janet adds before taking her notebook from her apron pocket and writes down another customer's order.

The rest of my day flies by faster than I wanted it too, and my nervous jitters have only gotten worse with every hour that passes. "I'll see you in the morning, Janet," I give my goodbye for the day and clock out. On the phone, she gives me a small wave. Stepping out the back door of the diner, waiting next to my car on his bike is Jake.

"Lead the way," he tells me.

No point in arguing, I get in my car. He's going to want answers. So, I need to make up my mind on the short fifteen-minute drive if I'm going to tell him the truth or feed him more lies.

Jake pulls in behind me as I put my car in park and turns off the engine. I'm out of the car and unlocking the front door just as he's walking up the drive. I open the door and walk straight to the kitchen needing a glass of water. I've yet to say a word to him even once he closes the door. Sipping my water, I try to calm my nerves.

I hear Jake sigh, "Grace."

"Give me a minute, Jake. I know you want answers. Give me a minute to gather the strength to give them to you," I plead. Setting my water down on the counter, I spin around but stay in the kitchen and face him. Jake starts striding my way, but I lift my hand, "I need you to stay right there. Please, Jake, because what I have to say is hard for me to reveal and harder for me to admit to you."

Noticing how visibly shaken I am, he stops and places his hands inside his front pockets—a move that instantly puts me at ease.

"I'm listening, babe," he remarks.

Pulling in a deep breath, I lay my secrets out in front of us. "My name isn't Grace Cohen," I bite my lip and rub my hands together nervously, and briefly look away.

"Eyes, Grace. Give me your eyes," Jake pleads in a calm, demanding tone.

My eyes meet his again.

"Keep going," he encourages me.

"I was born Anna O'Shea. I've been on the run, or I should say hiding for the past two years."

"Babe, what have you been running from?" Jake asks with worry etched across his handsome face.

"Not what but who." His eyes are soft, but change to rage with my admission, but still, he stays quiet. I close my eyes. This last part is the hardest to say to him. I'm not afraid of Jake. He would never hurt me physically. This I believe with every fiber in me. I'm afraid the last part I reveal will be me hurting him. I gather my strength and keep my eyes on his, "My married name is Anna De Burca, and I've been running from the man who almost killed me. I'm hiding from my husband." As hard as I try, I can't hold back my tears. I stand there letting them fall down my face, and I wait.

5

JAKE

"**I**'m hiding from my husband."

It's those five words that have all the air leaving my lungs and my vision seeing red. Hearing Grace's voice shake when she makes her confession has my fist clenching at my side. *Shit Jake, calm your ass down.* It's not the married part that's fucking with my head, because a quick bullet to the motherfucker's head will solve that problem. No, it's the fear in my Little Bird's eyes right now that has my anger soaring. I note the tremble in her body, and that alone is telling me she is afraid. She's scared of this bastard, fearful of opening up to me, and my gut is telling me I am not going to like what I am about to hear.

Keeping my emotions in check, I go against Grace's orders, and I take one, two, and three strides toward her until we are toe to toe. Reaching up, I cup her cheeks with my palms while relishing the feel of her silky skin on my rough, calloused hands. I watch as her eyes close, and she takes a shuttered breath before releasing it. "Tell me, Little Bird," I urge. Opening her eyes, she meets my stare.

"I'm scared," she confesses.

"I know you are, but you don't have anything to fear with me."

Digging her nails into my forearm while I keep my hold on her face, "The last time I allowed myself to get close to a man, it nearly killed me...literally," she chokes out.

"I would rather die than harm one hair on your gorgeous head, and I'd kill any motherfucker who dared to try," I say with conviction. Using the pad of my thumb, I swipe away the tears streaming down her face.

"I know you won't hurt me, Jake. I left because I was afraid," Grace whispers.

"I suspected as much, but make no mistake, Little Bird, you will be coming home with me. Consider your wings clipped." I feel her body tense at my words.

"You can't just show up and make demands, Jake. It doesn't work that way, not anymore. I refuse to have another man control me."

"I don't want to control you, Grace. I want to keep you safe, and the safest place for you is with me. Don't put me in the same category as that bastard because unlike him, everything I do will be for you. To make you safe and make you happy. You will always be my top priority." Hearing the truth in my statement, Grace closes her eyes tightly and nods. "First things first, though, is we are going to go sit down, and you are going to tell me as little or as much about what's happened to you. I won't force you to give me everything, at least not right now, but I need something from ya Grace."

Taking a deep breath, she agrees and leads me over to sit with her on the sofa. I sit down first, and Grace goes to sit at the other end, but I'm not having any of that so, not letting go of her hand, I pull her down to sit on my lap. "It's been six months since I've had my hands on you babe, I need you close." At my confession Grace's body melts into mine.

Chemistry is something we never had a problem with. We both have felt the pull toward each other from the moment we met; her hesitation is what had me treading carefully.

It takes Grace a few moments to collect herself before she begins to speak.

"Two years, ten months, and five days. That is how long I have been running from my husband. It was also the last time he beat me so bad I landed in the emergency room. It was not my first hospital visit, but it was the one where I met Finn, and he convinced me enough was enough. Detective Finn O'Rourke is the officer who took my statement at the hospital."

Grace must feel me tense underneath her, and she pauses to look at me. I run my hand up the length of her back encouraging her to continue.

"Anyway, my husband told Detective O'Rourke I had been mugged, but I could tell by the expression on Finn's face he wasn't buying it, and when my husband stepped out of the hospital room to take a phone call, Finn called me out on it. I didn't say a word to confirm nor deny his suspicions. I was too scared. Why would I have reason to trust another man, especially one I didn't know. That and my husband and his family are very powerful. Escaping was nearly impossible. I was watched twenty-four seven. I did escape, though, I took a chance that night and trusted Finn. He helped me escape my husband, and he's been helping me hide ever since. He found Polson for me and rented the space. The bakery, that was all him. A complete stranger. After a time, I got to know Finn and his reasoning for helping me and the way he makes complete sense now." Grace says the last statement with a somber tone. I'm also curious about what she means by her husband being powerful, but decide not to press. Not when she's finally opening up to me.

"I married Ronan when I was twenty-one, and in the time we

have been married, I have had two broken arms, a broken ankle, many fractured ribs and more black eyes and busted lips than I can count along with several concussions. All the while receiving pitied looks, people looking the other way. But what pissed me off the most were those who constantly asked; why do I stay, why don't I leave him."

Lightly gripping her hips to interrupt her, Grace looks at me. "You stayed because he would have killed you had you tried to leave."

With tears streaming down her face, she nods her head and then buries her face in the crook of my neck and sobs. I want Grace to know I would never judge her for staying in the situation she was in. Women who are in abusive relationships work strictly on fear and survival mode. I know in my heart that is what Grace was doing all those years she was with that soon-to-be a dead man. She was surviving. A little while later, her tears stop, and she looks up at me. Even with swollen red eyes and a tear-streaked face, she's still the most beautiful fuckin' woman. "No more storytellin' today, babe. You did good, and I'm proud of ya. Thank you for trusting me enough to give a part of yourself."

I pull her face toward mine, and my mouth comes crashing down on hers. It's been too long since I've had her taste on my lips. When I run my tongue over the seam of her lips, it is all the encouragement she needs to open up for me, and when she does, she lets me know she is just as starved for my taste as I am hers.

We kiss for what feels like forever; only forever is not long enough when it comes to this woman. In one swift movement, I grab Grace by the waist and shift her on my lap so that she is now straddling me. Her work uniform bunches up around her waist, and I can now feel the heat of her pussy against my dick which is straining against the zipper of my jeans, demanding to be released from its confines.

Grabbing a handful of Grace's red locks, I gently pull her away, and when I do the look on her face robs me of my words. Her swollen lips and lust-filled eyes are the most beautiful thing I have ever seen. "Tell me you want this baby. Tell me you're finally ready to become mine completely."

With a stunned look, she nods. "Words, Grace. Answer me with words," I demand.

"Yes, Jake, I want this. I'm ready."

Hearing all I need to understand, I swiftly stand from the couch with Grace still in my arms. With our bodies moving in sync, she bends her legs around my waist and wraps her arms around my neck. Striding toward the bedroom, not once do our eyes break their connection. Clearing the doorway of the bedroom, I kick it shut with my booted foot before making my way to the bed. Releasing Grace, her body slides down mine, and I don't miss the hitch in her voice when she feels my erection through my jeans. "Arms up, babe," I tell her, gripping the hem of her uniform. Complying, she raises her arms above her head allowing me to slip it off exposing her lace-covered breasts. Tossing her clothes to the floor, I then run my palms up the sides of her tits which are slightly more than a handful and hook my fingers into the cups of her white lace bra pulling them down.

My mouth waters at the sight of her dusty pink nipples, and it leaves me no choice but to go in for a taste. "Fuckin' perfect," I say just before my mouth is on her, taking her. Grace lets out a moan as I swirl my tongue around her nipple.

Fisting my hair, she arches her body into mine, and when she does, I award her other breast with the same attention. When my mouth leaves her body, she whimpers out my name.

"Jake."

Trailing soft kisses up her neck and behind her ear, to the place I know drives her wild, and she shivers. "Shh, baby. I'm going to take care of you," I say, unclasping her bra and letting it fall to the floor behind her. "Lay down on the bed."

Without a flicker of doubt, my brave woman does as I ask. The push and pull of the past two years have led us to this moment. Once Grace is laid out for me in nothing but a pair of white lace panties, I take a moment to ingrain this vision to memory. For a moment, I see a look of uncertainty cross her face. My pause has caused Grace to feel self-conscious, and she raises her arms to hide her body from me. "Don't ever hide your body from me, Grace. I only stopped because I want to take you in. I want to burn the vision of your gorgeous body into my brain." With a wicked grin, I drop down to the floor in front of the bed and lean back on my haunches.

Gripping Grace around her knees, I pull her to the edge of the bed, making my intention known. "It's time I get a taste of this sweet pussy you've been keeping from me. You don't know how many times I've jerked off to the thought of you ridin' my face." When I go to hook my thumbs into the waistband of her panties, Grace blurts out my name and covers her face. "What is it, babe? You want me to stop?" I ask.

"No," she answers quickly. "It's...nobody has ever done that to me, and my husband is the only man I've been with."

Taking a deep breath to tamp down my anger because the last thing I want to do right now is to talk about him, but I realize she's feeling nervous, and I need to calm her down. "Well, then I'm a lucky bastard because I'll be the first and last man ever to know what your pussy tastes like." At my declaration, our eyes lock in a heated gaze, and her body relaxes.

Moving forward, I continue with sliding her panties over her hips, exposing her small thatch of neatly trimmed hair. Once I have removed the last strip of clothing, I run my hands up the inside of her thighs pushing them open. One look at Grace's beautiful pussy wet with her desire and I can no longer hold back.

Without another second, I lean forward and swipe my tongue through her folds, stealing my first taste, the sensation causes Grace to cry out and her sweet sound fuels my need to make this experience the best. "Come for me, Grace," I growl just before I suck her clit.

"Oh god, Jake!" she screams, fisting my hair, and filling my mouth with her essence.

Emerging from between Grace's legs, I stand and reach behind me, pulling my shirt off over my head and use it to wipe my face and beard before adding it to the pile of clothes already on the floor. Peering down at my woman's sated body, I smile, "You taste like somethin' I've been missing for years, babe."

"What's that?" she asks.

"Forever. You taste like forever, Grace," I tell her honestly.

Shedding the rest of my clothes, I bring my body over the top of hers, and I don't miss the shocked look on her face when she looks down between us and gets her first look at my cock. I give her a knowing smirk when she visibly gulps. Laying my body flush against hers, I grind my heavy erection back and forth through her slick folds, and the feel of her heat has me almost coming. Leaning down further to where we are now chest to chest, I rest my forehead on hers. "I don't have a condom. This was not my intention when coming here. Please tell me I can take you bare, babe," I say, my control hangin' by a thread. "I'm clean, Grace. There hasn't been anyone since the moment I laid eyes on you." Seeing a flash of doubt cross her face, I continue, "I mean it, baby; it's only been you for over two years. No way was I going to stick my cock into anyone but you. And I knew it was going to be worth the wait." At my confession, Grace thrusts her hips upward, causing her wet pussy to rub against my cock and a deep growl to rumble in my chest.

"I'm clean too, and it's also been a while for me, but I'm not on anything, Jake," she says, thrusting once more.

CRYSTAL DANIELS & SANDY ALVAREZ

"I'll pull out. You good with that?" As soon as the word 'yes' leaves her mouth, I place one of her legs over my shoulder and wrap the other one around my waist. Then place the head of my cock at her entrance, and in one swift move, I bury myself balls deep as the room fills with the sounds of Grace's cries of pleasure mixed with the roar of mine.

Pausing for a moment not only for her to adjust to my size but also so I can gain some control over my body, so I don't come before we even start. A second later, I feel Grace's delicate hands slide up my chest and around my back, pulling me closer to her.

"I need to feel you. Please, Jake," she pleads.

Giving her what she asks for, I begin to move, sliding my shaft in and out of her tight heat with slow, purposeful strokes as the coarse hair on my chest rubs against her hardened nipples. With both of our bodies covered in sweat, I start to feel a familiar tingle at the base of my spine letting me know I won't be able to hold on much longer. Grinding my pelvis down, I connect with her clit, and the friction causes her pussy to spasm around my cock. "I want you to come for me one more time, Little Bird. Let me feel your sweet tight pussy come all over my cock." As soon as the command leaves my lips, Grace's pupils dilate, and her mouth opens as she screams out her orgasm.

Something I learned a long time ago is my shy timid woman loves my dirty mouth. No longer able to hold back my release, I reluctantly pull out of the sweetest pussy I've ever had, wrap my hand around my cock and pump. A few strokes later, jets of warm cum land all over Grace's pussy. I may not have come inside her, but I can still mark her as mine.

My body collapses next to hers; I pull her into my side, neither one of us saying a word for a few minutes. At this moment, words aren't needed. Grace knew this time was coming as well did I. We both know we have a lot more to tell each other. I know what Grace told me earlier about her past is only the tip of the iceberg, and I have yet to tap into things about my past. Grace knows I was married, and my wife passed away years ago, but I've never delved into any details. Maybe she never asked out of fear I would, in return, ask about her past. But something tells me that's not the case. I feel she will wait for me to tell her when I am ready.

Allowing myself to think about things, I believe Grace has been going slow with me the same way I have for her. Granted, her reasons are not entirely the same as mine.

"What are you thinking about so hard?" Grace's soft voice asks, bringing me out of my thoughts.

"I'm thinkin' about how I'm ready for us to move forward, how I want you in my life, in my home and my bed, and on the back of my bike. Are you ready to come home, Grace? Are you ready to trust that I can take care of you and that my club and I will do whatever necessary to protect you?" Twisting my body, so I am face to face with her, I cup her cheek and use my thumb to wipe away her tears. "The last six months have been killin' me, Little Bird. When you left, you took my soul with you. I love you, Grace." By the time I finish pouring my heart out, which is something I don't ever fuckin' do, but this woman has me by the damn balls. "Are you done running? Are you ready to come home?" I ask once more.

Grace pushes through her emotions, "Yes, I want to come home."

A couple of hours later, I'm lying in bed watching the rise and fall of Grace's chest. It's almost like my mind won't allow me to sleep, because if I do, I'll wake to find her gone. Shifting beside me, Grace rolls to her side, facing away from me and the sheet covering her body falls below her waist, exposing her bare shoulders and torso to me. And what I see peeking from beneath the sheet has all the air leaving my lungs. Scars. Some are so bad, the skin is slightly raised. Some are crisscrossed and some, then it dawns on me. *Fuck. Grace was whipped.* That's exactly what her back is covered in. Scars caused by someone taking what I'm guessing is a belt to her. Lifting the sheet, I let my eyes travel down and I see more of the same thing on her lower back. Dread settles in my stomach because I know at this moment that my woman, this beautiful, amazing and caring woman knows abuse.

6

GRACE

I lay in bed motionless as I feel Jake gently slide the sheets further down my body exposing my back. I hear the sharp intake of his breath as he takes in my scars from years of abuse. A lone tear falls down my cheek and across my upper lip when I feel his fingertip softly trace over my flesh. He pulls my body tight against his and wraps his strong protective arms around me. I take in a deep cleansing breath and soak in his warmth, thankful in the way he gives me the comfort I need without saying a single word.

Confessing so much of my past was easier than I thought it would be once I let the first few words cross my lips. Jake makes me feel safe in the way he handles himself. Giving me my space helped me feel like I wasn't backed into a corner with anywhere to go. However, I haven't told him all of it, and it is eating me up inside. I want so much to give him the whole story, but I'm hesitant about confiding in him completely. I'm holding onto a secret that may turn out to be a deal-breaker. I know what he wants. Jake has made his feelings known from the beginning. I know what I want too—happiness. I wish that with him. You would think I could rationalize all that has happened between us and move forward.

Instead, I feel stuck—my feet and hands bound tightly by my past and my fears.

Several hours later, I lay here on the couch, tucked into Jake's side, watching one of the two movies we picked up while in town earlier today, trying to muster the courage to finish telling him the rest of my story. He said he's staying for the weekend and wants me to come back to Polson with him tomorrow. I don't know if I can do that. I desperately want to believe he can and will love me forever. I'm so flustered with myself. I don't want to feel this way— all mixed up inside. I want Jake. I'll even admit I love him, just not out loud. I can't bring myself to say those three words he wants to hear. Not yet.

I need to take control of my life. I need to take back what Ronan had beaten out of me for years. Courage. Strength. I need to find myself. I count my breaths. I can do this. I'm ready to tell him everything.

Instead, I fall asleep.

Feeling my body become weightless, I open my eyes, and my face is buried in Jake's chest. Gripping his bare chest, I mumble something along the lines of, "I didn't mean to fall asleep."

Jake's chest ripples with a chuckle, "I was enjoying your soft snore too much to wake you," he tells me, carrying me down the hall.

I moan, "You were too warm. Your body heat was soothing." I smile as he places me on the bed. "What time is it?" I ask.

"Past midnight."

Crap. I slept right through my scheduled time to call Glory. I'll hear it in the morning. It's weird sharing my bed again. Snuggling is even more foreign. Ronan didn't like to be touched when he slept. Once he got what he wanted from me, he would roll over with his back to me and go to sleep. There was never any intimacy or physical connection between us before or after sex—not one bit of foreplay. Sometimes I got off. Most times, I didn't. I started to think something was wrong with me. Back when I had girlfriends, they talked about orgasms all the time. My friends boasted about their out of body experiences. It was never like that for me. I honest to God believed either my friends were stretching the truth, and the movies and many books I've read glorified the whole thing. Jake changed my entire perception of sex last night. Over the past two years, I've craved Jake's touch. I imagined how his large calloused hands would feel on my body. I feel my face heat just thinking about it. I swear he knows my body better than I remember it myself.

"Jake, I want to tell you something," I yawn so hard my eyes water.

"I'm sure it can wait until later, beautiful," he pulls the blankets over us and pulls my body against his. Wiggling, I find the nook of his body I was tucked against before. As I quickly drift back off to sleep, I hear Jake softly say, "I love you."

BOTH OF US are not in any hurry to leave the bed; we watch the morning sunbeams creeping across my bedroom wall. Silence hangs between us. Not because there isn't anything to say, but because so much can be said in a moment of silence. Before Jake leaves going back to Polson, I need to tell him what I planned on saying last night. Rolling to my side, I open my mouth, ready to lay everything out in the open.

My cell phone ringing breaks the silence. Reaching my arm across Jake's chest, I grab my phone from the nightstand. Only two people have my number. Sweeping my finger across the screen, I talk into the phone, "Hello."

"Anna." Glory's panic-filled voice vibrates in my ear.

"Glory, what's wrong?" I ask, cutting my eyes to Jake, whose face quickly morphs into concern.

"She's gone. Remi isn't here. I've been all over the house and even outside. I can't find her," her voice wails as she starts to cry.

My heart sinks like a brick to the bottom of my stomach. My first thought—*Ronan found her.* Darting out of bed, I start gathering my discarded clothes from the floor. My worst fears keep repeating themselves in my mind as I frantically slip some shoes on my feet.

"Grace, what the...Tell me what's happening, baby." Jake begins yanking his jeans on and slips his feet into his boots.

I run down the short hallway and snatch my purse from the counter and fumble, looking inside for my car key. Hot on my heels, Jake grabs my arm, stopping my forward motion as I head toward the front door. The move causes my body to freeze, and I have to remind myself this is Jake grabbing hold of me. I lift my head and look at him, tears pooling in my eyes.

"Slow down, Little Bird. Stop running, and tell me what's going on," he urges me, never letting go.

"I don't have time..." a light knock at my door stops my words of explanation. Before I can reach for the handle, Jake has my body tucked behind him and flings the door open. Jake's demeanor changes and I feel his body relax.

"Kind of early to be selling cookies?" Jake remarks, keeping me in place.

"I'm not a cookie pusher. I'm here to see my mom," the young voice sarcastically answers back.

"You got the wrong address, sweetheart," he quickly responds, at the same time I let out a gasp and cover my mouth in shock. Pushing Jake to the side, I brush past him.

"Oh my god! Remi, what the hell?" Relief washes over me as I embrace her.

She quickly wraps her arms around my waist and hugs me back, "I really wanted your homemade cinnamon rolls?" she jokingly replies. The girl can't take anything seriously. Most of the time, I look past her humor because that's how she deals with stress, but I can't ignore it this time. All joking aside, I pull back and give her a stern look. "What the hell were you thinking? Your aunt just called frantic to the point of hyperventilating." Remi hangs her head for a moment to hide her face. Scolding her isn't something I like to do, but I won't tolerate this type of behavior from her, and she knows it. Lifting her head, she opens her mouth with what I assume is an apology. Instead, she looks over my shoulder and smirks.

"Who's the guy, Mom?"

Oh, my God, I forgot about Jake. I plant my face in the palm of my hand.

"Wait," she pauses, "Is this Jake? You know the biker guy you and Aunt Glory talk about all the time." Remi continues to stare past me.

Heat spreads across my cheeks. Turning, I face Jake and pull Remi into my side, "Remi, this is Jake." Letting a brief pause hang in the air, I release the next words on an exhale, "Jake, meet Remi; my daughter."

Sighing heavily, he runs his hand through his hair, quickly trying to process the significant bombshell that landed in his lap. I was planning on telling him. This morning, as a matter of fact. I damn sure didn't want him to find out like this. I grab my daughter's hand, close the door and lead her to sit on the couch. Removing her backpack, she drops it to the floor and plops down. I wish Jake would say something. Anything. I sit next to my daughter and hold her hand. "Jake, I'm sorry. Let me explain," my voice trembles with fear that he will leave. Reading me like an open book, he calms my nerves.

"I'm not going anywhere, and you and I can talk about this later. I know you have your reasons, Little Bird." Striding to the kitchen, Jake opens the fridge, grabbing a soda from inside. Walking back, he hands it to Remi. She cranes her neck, looking at him and gives him a small glare—her attempt to intimidate him.

"You like my mom?" she continues her stare.

I do my best to hide my smile and suppress a giggle caused by her behavior. She may look like me, but that's as far as it goes. Remi has fire and grit. I'm all for her speaking her truth and expressing herself as long as she is respectful about it. She reminds me a lot of my own mother.

Jake, however, doesn't hide his amusement, which doesn't go over too well with my overprotective daughter. Letting go of my hand, she crosses her arms and throws herself into the back of the couch. I can tell Remi is slightly nervous when she begins to twirl her hair with her fingers. She doesn't know how to take Jake, and like me, she doesn't trust people. "How did you get here, Remi?" I finally ask her.

Like it's no big deal, my daughter shrugs. "A bus. There was one leaving super early this morning. I made sure it would make it here before Aunt Glory found me missing," she looks at me, "I left her a note."

"Well, unfortunately, she didn't see it. Either way, you're twelve years old. You can't go hopping buses at midnight whenever you please. Where did you get the money for a bus ticket anyway?" I continue to grill her. Dammit, she knows better than this.

She sighs, "I took money from Aunt Glory's wallet, but I promise I'll pay it back somehow," she quickly confesses.

"Damn right, you will young lady. You may not have the ideal life right now, but you've never wanted for anything. I didn't raise you to steal," I scold her.

"Two years, Mom. **TWO.** I want to be with you." My heart breaks with every word she says.

"Your dad is still out there looking for us. At least this way, if he finds me, he won't find you, Remi. I don't like it either. I'm only keeping you safe the best way I know how." Throwing herself into my arms, my daughter buries her face in my chest. I hate the pain she's feeling. *I feel it too.* Sniffling, she pulls away, "Mom, I'm really tired. I haven't slept for hours." Remi wipes at her eyes with the sleeve of her cotton hoodie.

"Okay, come with me. While I put some fresh sheets on the bed, you can call your aunt and let her know you're alright and apologize for the money. Got it?" I stand her up and lead her to my room. I pause next to Jake, who hasn't interrupted or said a word.

"Take care of your daughter first, then come talk to me. I'm gonna step outside for a minute," Jake informs me.

With a weak smile, I turn away and lead Remi to the extra room down the hall.

"I know. I'm sorry," Remi says to Glory on the phone, while I finish making up the small twin bed for her. Ending the call, my daughter stands from sitting cross-legged on the floor. The small bedroom only has a bed in it because it's the size of a closet. Nothing else could fit in here if you tried.

"I'm sorry there's no TV in here, Peanut," I tell her.

Climbing under the cover, she lays her head on the pillow, "I've got my phone. My music is all I need," she yawns again.

Reaching out, I brush my fingers through her hair like I have since she was born and sigh, "Promise me you won't go and do something stupid like this again," I tell her.

"I'm twelve. I've got years of poor decisions to make."

I give her a look. We all know the 'Mom' look. The one that says you'd better check yourself. The one where she draws the line and dares you to cross it.

"Fine. I promise," she says, rolling her eyes.

"Get some sleep. I'll see if Jake will run to the store for me. I'll cook you those cinnamon rolls you were so eager to have," I kiss her forehead.

Smiling, she closes her eyes. "Thanks, Mom."

I leave her room, closing the door behind me and walk outside to find Jake sitting in the one plastic lawn chair right outside my front door. "Hey," I whisper.

"Come here," Jake pulls me to sit on his lap. "She looks just like you, freckles and all."

"Jake, I'm sorry. I was planning on telling you this morning."

"Two years, babe. That's a hard pill to swallow..."

Before he finishes with what I assume is rejection, I interrupt him, "I understand if this changes everything. I lied. A lot. I can't say that I'm sorry. I did all of it to protect her. I'd do it again in a heartbeat," I rush to say in my defense.

"Look at me," Jake demands his voice rough and raw withheld back emotions. "She's not a deal breaker. Allow me to feel and process all this, but know I'm not runnin' away. I want us. Remi is yours, so that now makes her mine, Little Bird. I know you've been through a lot, and I know it will take time, but you have to learn I'm nothing like that piece of shit you married."

He's right. Jake is nothing like Ronan.

Calm washes over me. Deciding it's now or never, I choose to follow my heart. Placing my palm on his cheek, I tell him, "I love you."

7

JAKE

I wake the next morning to the smell of coffee and the sounds of Grace shuffling around in the kitchen. Sitting up on the sofa, I toss the blanket aside and stifle a yawn with my fist. With Grace's daughter showing up yesterday, I felt it was best to sleep out here in the living room.

The kid is smart, and I believe she suspects her mother and I are together, but I have enough respect for my woman and her daughter to set some boundaries until we've had a chance to talk with her and see where her head is at on everything that is going on. The last thing I want is to start on the wrong foot with Remi and ruin any chance of building some trust with her.

Finding out Grace has a kid has thrown me for a fuckin' loop. I'm not mad at her for not telling me, though. I agree one hundred percent with the decision she made with Remi. I can't imagine the pain she must have been going through the past couple of years, not having her daughter with her, not seeing her every day. A parent will go through hell and suffer to keep their child from harm, and that is exactly what Grace has done. Seeing how brave and strong she is has made me love her more than I already do if that's even possible.

And on top of all that, Grace assumed her having a daughter and keeping it secret would be a deal breaker for me. I told her yesterday it wasn't, but I intend to talk with her this morning to make myself clearer. I don't want her to have a shred of doubt in her head about my feelings on the situation.

"I didn't mean to wake you, I'm sorry," Grace apologizes in a hushed tone. Standing, I stretch my arms over my head to work out some of the soreness from my back from sleeping on the sofa, and I don't miss Grace's heated look when I go to retrieve my t-shirt off the table in front of me. Clearing my throat brings her attention away from my body and to my face. "Like what you see, Little Bird?" I ask with a smirk. I'm rewarded with an eye-roll, and I don't miss the slight blush of her cheeks before she turns around and proceeds to fix herself a cup of coffee. After I slip my shirt back on, I stand here a moment and look at my woman and admire her beauty, and all that is Grace. I'm a lucky bastard to have found this woman.

Striding up behind Grace, I press my body flush against her back while sweeping her fiery red hair away from the nape of her neck and kiss her gently below her ear. And I purposely grind my erection against her back, letting her know the effect she has on me. "Good mornin', Grace," I rasp.

"Morning," she breathes in return.

"Fix me a cup, would ya? I'm going to hit the head," I say, giving her another kiss.

Grabbing my overnight bag from by the front door, I make my way to the bathroom to take care of business. Once I have brushed my teeth and washed my face, I stride back out into the kitchen to where Grace is sitting at the table, drinking her coffee, and I take notice of her fidgeting. Taking a seat across from her, I casually pick up my cup and quietly sip on it while waiting for her to speak what's on her mind. After several moments I decide to be the one to break the silence. "You want to tell me what's on your mind, babe?" Tucking a lock of curls behind her ear and straightening her back, Grace opens her mouth, closes it, and then opens it again. "I'm not sure if I should come back to Polson. I haven't even decided what to do about Remi. I'm scared to keep her with me, but at the same time, I'm terrified she'll pull another stunt like she did yesterday. I'm a mess, Jake."

"The answers are easy, babe. You and Remi will be coming home with me. We already discussed this yesterday. The plan hasn't changed."

"Jake, I have my daughter to think about." Setting my cup down, I cut her off, "I'm thinking about her too, both of you. Can you honestly sit there and tell me you know of a safer place for the two of you than in Polson with me? Are you prepared to send her back to Glory while you keep running from one town to the next? It's time to get your life back, Grace, you and Remi." Grace's daughter showing up may be working in my favor. Not that I wouldn't have gotten her to come home with me regardless, because I would have tossed her over my shoulder and tied her ass on the back of my bike if need be, but now with Remi in the picture, it makes my convincing Grace easier.

The second I see her shoulders slump and she expels a heavy sigh, I know there is no more arguing. "You're right, Jake, it's time to try and move forward and quit running. Now I need to talk with Remi. She wants us back together; I don't think she cares where we go so long as she can come. I'm going to assume you want to leave soon, but I'd like to stop by the diner and talk to my boss before leaving. She's been good to me, and I don't want to go without saying goodbye. And I don't have much to pack, just my clothes. I'm going to go take a shower before Remi wakes up, then I'll make us some breakfast," Grace rambles off.

"Babe," I say, getting her attention. "Breathe. Everything is going to be fine."

Remi appears from the hallway in rumpled pajamas and rubbing her sleep-filled eyes. "Morning, Peanut. How'd you sleep?" Grace asks, standing from the table and going to her daughter. Looking at the two of them side by side, I see how remarkably identical their looks are. Remi is a carbon copy of her mom. She has the same blue eyes, same red curly hair, and the same freckles. She is Grace made over.

"Babe, why don't ya go on and take your shower, and I'll cook breakfast," I say, giving Grace and Remi a warm smile.

"You're going to cook?" Remi asks with a shocked look on her face.

Confused by her reaction, I go to answer her, but Grace beats me to it, and what she says has me understanding her daughter's question. "Remi, Jake is not like *him*. I promise," she tells her daughter in a hushed tone. I don't need to hear more to know what she is talking about. Grace's daughter is not used to seeing a man do what some may call a woman's job. I sit here and silently grind my teeth at the thought of the motherfucker who has poisoned this innocent child's mind. She has no idea how a real man acts and treats those he loves and cares for.

Standing from my seat at the table, I walk over to the sink, placing my cup inside. I stand here briefly so I can get my anger under control before I turn my attention back to Grace and her daughter. "How about I whip up some pancakes? You like pancakes, don't ya, sweetheart?" I ask Remi. Looking at her mother, then back at me when Grace gives her a reassuring nod, Remi answers, "Yes, sir, I love pancakes. Do you know how to make them?"

I give her a playful glare, "Of course I do. Maybe not as good as your momma does, but I used to make them all the time for my nephew, Logan. Come on, you can help," I coax and don't miss the beaming smile on Grace's face when her daughter, without hesitation, opens the refrigerator door and proceeds to gather the ingredients needed. Trusting me with Remi, Grace quietly leaves the room and heads in the direction of the bathroom to take her shower. As I'm opening and closing several cabinets looking for a skillet, Remi asks. "Do you still cook for your nephew?"

"Nah, sweetheart. Not for a long time. Logan is grown now," I chuckle.

"Oh," she says with slight disappointment. When I mentioned a nephew, she probably was expecting a kid, maybe someone her age. "He and his wife Bella have a daughter, though. Breanna is six months old now." Remi perks up at the news. "Really!"

"Really. There's also Sofia, and she's eighteen. Then we have Reid and Mila and their daughter Ava who is five. Then there is Gabriel and his wife, Alba. They have two children, Gabe is two, and Val is not even one yet."

"Wow! You have a big family."

"I do. You'll get to meet them as soon as we get back to Polson. You'll like them, and they'll love you. I hope you're ready for endless amounts of shopping. I'm sure Bella and Alba will kidnap ya whenever possible and drag you to all their favorite stores."

"I'd like that," she says, ducking her head, but I don't miss the big smile taking over her face. Over the next several minutes, we go about cooking breakfast in comfortable silence. I catch Remi, always cutting her eyes over at me like she's studying me. Like she's still not quite sure what to make of this big tattooed biker standing in her mom's kitchen making her breakfast. Once I have placed our food on our plates, I motion for Remi to take a seat at the table. I wait for her to sit before I follow suit. I pass her the syrup for her to use first. "You can use it first," she says quietly. Shaking my head no, I reply, "Ladies first, sweetheart." We are both halfway through our meal before I decide I can no longer bite my tongue. Remi's father had no doubt poisoned her mind. I want her to know that the men she will soon meet and I are not chauvinistic pricks. Remi and I don't know each other so I could try and talk to her and convince her that I am different, but because we are strangers, I can talk till I am blue in the face, and it wouldn't do any good. As they say, actions speak louder than words. So, I will have to show her with my actions. I will have to work on gaining her trust. Deciding I need to see where her head is on things and how she is feeling about her current situation, I ask. "Did your momma tell you about going back to Polson? How do you feel about that?"

"She talked to me last night when she was putting me to bed. I want to be where my mom is. Besides, I know she likes it there, and she loves the bakery." Fidgeting in her seat a moment, something she gets from Grace when something is on her mind, I wait patiently for her to speak it. "I've heard my mom talking to my Aunt Glory about you. She likes you."

"Well, I would hope so because I like your mom," I say with a wink, and that earns me a giggle. "Look, I get the feeling you're a smart kid, so I'm going to lay it all out for ya. I care for your mom very much. I want to protect her and make her happy. And because you are a part of her, I want to do all those things for you too. Now, I am not going to ask you to trust me, because you don't know me. But what I am going to ask you is to give me a chance. A chance to show you I mean what I say, and I say what I mean. I'm a man who will go to the ends of the earth to protect the people I care about. Your mother is a queen, and she will be treated as such." Not used to hearing someone speak so highly of her mom, Remi stares at me with a stunned look on her face, then quickly recovers and offers me a big smile. "Do we have a deal?" I ask, holding out my hand. Placing her small hand in mine, we shake, and she answers, "Deal."

"Good, now let's finish eating. We have a long day ahead of us." We finish eating our breakfast, and I breathe a sigh of relief and celebrate my small victory.

8

GRACE

In a few hours, I'm heading back to Polson with my daughter and Jake. To say I'm slightly nervous is an understatement. For two years, I've built relationships with everyone in town, especially Bella, and for those two years, I've been living a lie. On the surface, I worry they will hate me, but deep down in my heart, I know they aren't like that. My friends are the least judgmental group of people I know.

Then there's Glory. Glory Keller has been my best friend since I was eight years old. If she wasn't with me at my house, I was at hers. Glory's family is very wealthy, but you would never know it because they aren't the kind of people who go about showing it off. We were inseparable. She's also the only person allowed to call me Anna anymore. Little by little, I had fewer communications with the people I loved. I noticed a change in Ronan. He was becoming more irritable, and extremely suspicious of everyone around him, to the point we stopped going to family dinners on Sunday, and he also started having an issue with the time I would spend with Glory. Before I knew it, he had control over every facet of my life.

Over time I began to notice all the dirty secrets the De Burca family kept neatly tucked away from outsiders. It got to the point Ronan didn't try to hide the filthy and illegal things he and his 'employees' were up to. I've heard him threatening the lives and livelihoods of so many people I stopped counting. I remember the first time I witnessed him, and one of his men beat another man near death. I wanted to turn and leave the room, but Ronan ordered me to stay. He wanted me to see what happens to people who didn't do as they were told.

I became a prisoner in my own home. Things got worse once I became pregnant with Remi. Fear of him hurting me and causing harm to my baby had me complying with every command he made. I hide the fact I was keeping in touch with Glory after my mom died for some time until he found a cell phone I had kept secret from him. Remi was three then. That was the first time he ever hit me in front of my daughter.

"Babe, we need to hit the road soon so that we can make it before sunset," Jake walks up behind me and rests his chin on my shoulder then kisses my neck. The contact instantly causes my skin to prickle.

"Okay. Let me give Glory a call before we leave," I tell him.

"I'll be out front when you get done." He gives me a reassuring squeeze and walks away.

Pulling my phone from my back pocket, I give my best friend a call. It rings a few times before she picks up.

"Hey," Glory says, her voice sounding tired.

"You sound exhausted. Still not sleeping well?" I ask, feeling concerned.

"When have I ever? Insomnia has run my life for years. I think I'd freak out if I slept for more than two hours straight," she laughs, trying to play it off. It's true. Ever since she was a teenager, she has had insomnia. I sleep like a log, so I can't imagine running on empty all the time as she does. "Well, I'm packed. We should be pulling out and heading to Polson in about thirty minutes. I wanted to give you a call before getting on the road," I tell her.

"I'm so happy you decided to go back to Polson. Jake sounds like a good guy, and he will do anything it takes to protect you and Remi," she admits.

"You going to be okay by yourself? You've had her company for the past two years," I tell her.

"I'll miss her presence, but Remi is right where she needs to be; with you," Glory quickly responds.

"I promise to call you once we've gotten settled." I sigh and flip the last light switch off in the apartment before stepping outside.

"You'd better," she mocks in a motherly tone, "and tell Remi I love her," she says somberly, which leads me to believe the adjustment of being alone in an empty home will be harder than she realizes.

"I can hear your thoughts. Stop it. I have Bo to keep me company," she says. Bo is her overgrown basset hound.

"I love you. I'll talk to you soon."

"Ditto. Drive safe."

She ends the call, and I shove my phone back into my pocket. With my keys in my hand, I lock the door to the duplex. As the landlord suggested, I walk next door and knock. He asked that I leave my keys with my neighbor, who also happens to be his grandson. Chris opens the door, greeting me with a smile.

"Hi, Grace. Leaving, huh?" He rubs the back of his neck with his hand and quickly glances toward Jake, who is mounting his bike.

"Yeah. Please give these to your grandad and tell him thank you for me." I reach into my bag and pull out an envelope. "And this is the two weeks rent I owe him."

"Sure. You take care of yourself, Grace," Chris says with a slight smile.

"You too," I tell him and make my way to my car, where my daughter is waiting for me in the front seat. Climbing in, I throw my bag into the back seat. "Put your seatbelt on, Peanut," I instruct my daughter who complies along with a dramatic sigh. Once Jake makes way for me, I back out and head toward the diner.

Before leaving town, I need to swing by and say goodbye to Janet. I called her yesterday—a call I found out she was expecting to let her know I would be quitting. I was worried I would be leaving her in a tight spot but turns out her daughter is moving back home with her grandchild in a few days and would need a job, so the whole situation worked out perfectly.

I pull into the parking lot a few minutes later and Jake pulls in beside me. "I won't be but a minute." I turn and address my daughter, "You want anything for the road while we're here? It will be a while before stopping again."

She puts her earbuds in, "I'm good, Mom."

The door chimes the moment I open it, and Janet is standing behind the register handing a receipt with the change to a guy, so I stand off to the side and wait for her.

"Grace," she gives me a motherly hug. "I hate to see you go, hon, but you and I both know you were never happy here. I think your heart was always somewhere else."

Giving her a knowing smile, I hand her my uniform. "You've helped me more than you know, Janet. I'm going to miss you."

Janet reaches into the pocket of her apron and pulls out a folded envelope containing my last paycheck. "I see my daughter in you. Let's say she's a survivor too." Janet passes the envelope to me, and I tuck it in my back pocket. I'm not going to meddle. I know how to read between the lines as to what she is referring to. I've overheard more than one phone call between her and her daughter and the desperation in her pleading voice every time. I give her a final hug goodbye. "Your daughter is fortunate to have you."

"And you and that man out there on the motorcycle are lucky to have each other," she replies.

On her final words, I leave. I walk up to Jake, "She's a good woman." I turn and look back at the diner. Laying his hands on my hips, Jake pulls me in.

"I know, babe. She and I had a little chat the day I came in looking for you."

Surprised by his admission, I raise my brow and wait for him to elaborate.

"She pretty much told me she'd chop my balls off if I hurt ya," he chuckles, then plants a kiss on my smiling lips. Swatting my butt, he tells me to get in the car. Noticing my daughter is in her own little world filled with music as she plays a game on her phone, I put the car in drive and turn onto the highway heading east.

After a few hours, we make a quick stop at a rest area inside the Montana state line. I give Remi a few dollars to grab herself some vending machine snacks, and we hit the road once again. Deciding now is as good a time as any, I decided to talk to her about Jake and me. Reaching across the console, I tug on the earbud in her left ear to grab her attention. She taps the screen of her phone and turns her face toward me, giving me her full attention.

"What's up?" She speaks softly.

"I want to talk to you about Jake. I want to know what's going on inside that head of yours."

She's quiet for a moment. "I feel okay about Jake. He makes you smile, and I like that," she says, smiling herself.

I smile back, "I like that too."

"He has kind eyes, and when he talked to me yesterday, he made me feel safe. Dad always made me feel small and scared all the time. Jake was easy to talk to." Turning her head, she looks out the window at the passing fence posts on the side of the road, "Do you love him like you used to love Dad?" she asks.

"I love him more," I confess to my daughter.

Her focus lands back on me, this time, her expression raw with emotions, "Does he love you too? Like really love you?"

I take her hand in mine. "Yes, Peanut, Jake loves me," I assure her. Both finding comfort in the small conversation we held, Remi digs her stash of candy from her bag and holds it out for me to dip my hand in. For the rest of the ride, we eat junk food and sing along to the radio. That one little mother-daughter moment in a sense is freeing for both of us.

With the Polson exit up ahead, Jake passes my car and takes the lead. Taking the street leading away from the town, I follow him through winding roads for several miles. The people who live out this way are spread out from one another. Slowing Jake's turn signal starts flashing as he turns on a blacktop road. We cross over a stone bridge where a small creek runs before his home comes into view.

I take in the beautiful cabin appearing at the end of the road. The one thing that stands out the most is the front porch. It's a huge wrap-around and expands the entire home.

Remi gasps, "Mom, look, horses," she points out to my left. Sure enough, two horses are standing near a fence line off in the distance. "Do you think he'd let me pet them?" she scoots forward on her seat.

Laughing, I tell her, "I'm not even sure they belong to him, Peanut, but you can ask." Jake parks his bike in front of a large shed, so I pull up beside him. As soon as I stop, Remi unbuckles and bolts out the door. Before I have my door fully open, she's bouncing on her toes, waiting for Jake while he opens the large shed doors and pushes his motorcycle inside.

"Are those horses yours?" Remi shuffles from foot to foot.

He looks off toward the wooden fence where the horses are grazing. "Sorry, sweetheart. They aren't mine. I allow a friend of mine to let them graze on my land. They're pretty docile if you want we can go visit them tomorrow morning," he explains, and her face lights up.

"Can I see them in the morning, Mom?" my daughter begs.

"I don't have a problem with it as long as Jake or I am with you," I inform her and lift my eyes to Jake's.

"Alright, ladies, let me give you the penny tour of the place tonight," Jake offers, and we start walking in the direction of the front door. Punching in the code, his door unlocks, and Remi and I step inside. It's as beautiful inside as it is outside. The first room we enter is the living room. It's like walking into the pages of a magazine. His furniture is mostly brown leather, but the whole place doesn't appear too dark with the large windows, and light gray paint on the walls. I can't wait to see the room basked in light from the rays of sun pouring in during the day. He leads us to a separate kitchen, and I stop because I'm standing in my dream kitchen. Jake spared no expense with the high-end stainless appliances along with light gray, granite countertops. "You have all this, and it looks like you never use it," I remark as I open the convection oven big enough to cook three pans of just about anything.

"Never needed to. I like to cook, but it's just me out here. Come on. I'm going to show you your rooms."

"Mom, look," Remi points out the large bay window on the other side of the room. "Is that a river back there?"

Jake answers, "You're looking at part of Flathead River."

CRYSTAL DANIELS & SANDY ALVAREZ

"Wow," Remi responds.

Climbing the stairs to the top floor of the home, Jake continues to show us around. "There's a bathroom here," he opens the door and turns the light on, "the towels and everything you guys will need is in the cabinets." I allow my gaze to drift. Brand new bottles of bubble bath and woman's shampoo sit on the edge of the enormous tub.

"Remi," Jake takes a few steps down the hall and opens another door, "this is your room. If you don't like anything, let me know, and we can redecorate it," he tells her.

As eager as my daughter, we step inside to a fully decorated bedroom any teenage girl would love to have. Remi isn't a girly girl, so it's perfect. It's done in soft creams, whites, and grays. Strings of sparkly lights drape across the high wooden headboard, and a plush hammock chair hangs in the corner with a round, shag gray carpet splayed underneath it, creating the perfect nook. My daughter stands frozen, while her eyes peer around the room. When she looks at me with tears pooling in her eyes, I almost lose it myself. Walking to her, I wrapped my arms around her, and she buries her face into my chest. I stroke her hair a few times and kiss the top of her head. I lift my head to where Jake is quietly observing by the bedroom door, and I lip a thank you to him.

"You want to hang out here for a few minutes?" I ask Remi. She answers with a couple of sniffles and a nod. I release her, and she shocks me by walking up to Jake and wrapping her arms around his waist. He doesn't hesitate to hug her back. Releasing him, she beelines it to the swing. I leave her to explore her room and stop Jake before he opens the other bedroom door a couple of feet from where we are standing. "Thank you. You just made a big impact on her; on both of us." Gripping his arms, I tiptoe to kiss him. He meets me halfway and softly kisses my lips. I press my body into his and deepen the kiss.

"I don't know how you did it, but the room is beautiful, Jake," I say breathlessly.

"Come on, let me show you the other room." He grabs my hand, leading the way. The second bedroom is as stunning as Remi's. Decorated in a white and blue scheme with a large queen bed.

"I called Logan and had him send the women shopping for you and Remi. Everything you could need is here. I even had them buy a few clothes. I'm pretty sure they had an easier time shopping for you, but with Remi, all they had to go on was my description of her. If she doesn't like anything, we'll take it back," he tells me in one breath. We walk across the hallway.

"This is the master bedroom." Jake slides two heavy barn doors open that hang from tracks on the wall. One whole half of the upstairs is his bedroom. The first thing you notice is the oversized king bed centered under windows that span the length of the room and reach as high as the vaulted ceiling. The place isn't massive, but the windows make it feel open. He kept the large beams in the ceiling exposed as he did downstairs, and it's beautiful.

I'm speechless for a moment as I take in how much my friends care, and I let everything sink in. Jake is offering me a home—his home. He's proving he wants to provide for my daughter and me.

Jake steps behind me, as I'm standing there collecting my thoughts. "I didn't want to assume, so the second spare room I showed you is for you."

"Me?" I turn and face him, not hiding the sting from his words.

He grabs my face in the palm of his hands. "I want nothing more than to have you in **our** room and **our** bed with me, Little Bird, but I want the choice to be yours."

Understanding where he is going with his choices, I sigh and bury my face in his chest. "I can't thank you enough, Jake."

"No thanks needed, beautiful. You and Remi are mine now. I

don't want to take your choices away from you. There's nothing I won't do to make sure you both always feel safe and loved as you deserve."

"I love you," I whisper and kiss him just under his ear.

Jake lifts me off my feet, "I love you too, Little Bird."

9

JAKE

Waking up the next morning with Grace in my bed and my home is the best fuckin' feeling in the world. When we got home yesterday evening, I decided I would wait and see what choice Grace was going to make. I have three bedrooms in my house. I had both spare rooms furnished, and I showed both to Grace. I made it clear the decision was hers to make. Did I want my woman in my bed with me? Hell yes, but having her under my roof was also a win. I was going to take what I could get.

Tucking Grace tighter into me, she lets out a small whimper while wiggling her ass into my erection. My dick has been hard as a fuckin' rock ever since she climbed into my bed last night. I wanted to take her then, especially since all she had on was a t-shirt and panties. But I knew she was worn out from the long-ass drive yesterday, so I kept my dick under wraps.

This morning though, my cock has other plans, and those plans are gettin' inside my woman's hot as fuck pussy. Rolling slightly away from Grace's warm body, I go about removing my boxer briefs. I then begin to pepper kisses on her exposed shoulder where her sleep shirt has slipped, giving me access. At the same time, I reach my right hand down and gently tug her panties down over her hips. I don't miss the slight rock of Grace's body, alerting me that she is awake and is aware of my intentions as she aids in helping me remove the scrap of material from her body. Once her pussy is bare to me, I run my fingers through her slit finding she is already soaked for me. "You're ready for me, aren't ya babe?" I growl, and she hums in response as she places her own hand on the top of mine and urges my hand to move. "That's it Little Bird, show me what you want."

With my encouragement, Grace opens her legs wider for me, and with her hand still on mine, she guides my fingers back and forth through her wet pussy. With my hand between her legs and my cock against her ass, our bodies rock together in a perfect rhythm. I'm so close to the fuckin' edge, and I can't wait another second to be inside her. When my hand leaves her body Grace whimpers in protest. After ridding her of her t-shirt and exposing her perfect tits, I roll her onto her stomach as I settle my body in behind her spread legs. "Ass out, babe," I demand, taking a pillow and placing it underneath her hips. "Now, put your arms out in front of you and hold on to the headboard." Without a word, Grace continues to do as I ask. With her breaths coming out in pants, Grace turns her head and looks at me with hooded eyes. We hold each other's stare as I grip the sides of her hips and slowly sink into her tight heat. Once I'm fully seated, I lean forward and grasp the headboard right above where Grace has her hands. With my large body cocooned around her much smaller one and my face a mere inch from hers, I begin to thrust. Soon Grace's heavy pants turn into moans and she buries her face in the pillow to muffle her cries of pleasure. "Mouth," I order when I feel my balls draw up and her pussy begins to ripple around my cock. With our tongues battling each other, I pick up my pace. "God damn it," I grind out breaking our kiss. "I'll never get enough of your pussy."

"I'm coming, Jake."

"I know, I can feel it. Your pussy is greedy for my cock, isn't it, Grace?"

"Yes, yes, yes," she chants over and over as I drill harder into her. And when her mouth opens, I bring mine crashing down on it once again, swallowing her orgasm as I still inside of her, allowing myself to follow while her tight heat milks every drop of cum from my body.

Once I've recovered, I raise off Grace and curse myself when I pull out of her. "Fuck."

Craning her neck, she asks, "What? Is everything okay?"

"I'm sorry, babe, I got caught up in the moment."

Scrunching her brows in confusion and pulling the sheet up to cover herself, she asks, "What are you talking about, Jake?"

Scrubbing my hand down my face, "I forgot to use a condom. I fucked up."

"Jake, I told you I wasn't on birth control." We both stay silent, gauging each other's reaction. I can't help the smile that comes over my face at the thought of Grace round with my baby. "Jake!" Grace screeches, drawing my attention. "What the hell are you smiling for? This is serious."

"I wouldn't mind having a baby with you, Little Bird," I confess, shrugging my shoulders.

"Oh god," Grace groans, face planting into the bed.

"Babe, look at me." Grace refuses, shaking her head 'no' while snatching the pillow and covering her face with it. "Yes. Look at me, Little Bird." At my last plea, she peeks out from behind the pillow. "We'll take this one day at a time, okay? I know your life has been turned upside down, but I promise I'm not going anywhere, and neither are you. Whatever happens, we'll get through it." Pushing the pillow away, Grace gets up onto her knees, and I pull her into my chest and rest my chin on top of her head. "One day at a time, babe."

"You're right, besides I don't blame you. Using protection is as much my responsibility as it is yours. I got lost in the moment too. It's both our faults."

I don't know how long Grace and I sit in the middle of the bed, holding each other, but we are both brought out of our fog when we hear the opening and closing of the bathroom door telling us Remi is up. "I better get up, so I can make some breakfast," Grace announces. When she makes a move to get out of bed, I tighten my hold on her, halting her movements.

"Before you do, there's something else we need to talk about." Grace looks at me expectantly waiting for me to elaborate. "I need to ask you about Ronan." As soon as her husband's name leaves my mouth, her body goes rigid. "I don't want to talk about you and him. I know you'll finish that story when you're ready. What I want to discuss is him—his story. I've called church for later today. The club is going to handle the situation. It's time for this shit to be over once and for all, Grace."

"What are you going to do?"

Without sugar coating it, I answer her question. "I'm gonna kill him."

"You're serious?" she chokes out.

"As a fuckin' heart attack."

"Maybe we should let Finn handle the situation. I already told you his family is powerful. I doubt you'd ever get close enough to him to carry out your threat. Ronan doesn't go anywhere without his men."

"O'Rourke has to play by the rules, babe. I don't. He has to wait for Ronan to slip before he can do anything. It's been two years, and the bastard hasn't done anything to give the police a reason to arrest him. O'Rourke knows the fucker is after you, and if he finds you, then he would most likely kill you. He can't put him behind bars without evidence of him doing anything. You get that, don't ya?"

With a defeated sigh, Grace nods. "Yeah, I know how the law

works, Jake. I don't want you to get in trouble or get caught all because of me. If something happens to you, I wouldn't be able to live with myself. I can't lose you, Jake. I just got you." Burying her face in my neck, Grace begins to sob, her fear for me making my gut twist.

"You have nothing to worry about, Grace. Believe it or not, I know what I'm doing. If it makes you feel better, I'll put a call into O'Rourke and see if there have been any new developments since he's been back to Chicago."

Snapping her head up, Grace asks, "What do you mean since he's been back in Chicago? I never told you where Finn was from."

"I know all about Finn O'Rourke, babe. My boys and I ran into him at your apartment above the bakery. He was there, making sure you cover your tracks. After the informative conversation we had with him, I had Reid check him out."

"That's how you knew where to find me, isn't it?" she asks.

"He didn't come right out and tell me, but he gave me enough to figure it out on my own. I would have eventually found you, babe, with or without his help."

"I'm going to kill him the next time I see him," she huffs.

"O'Rourke made the right call, and you know it. As I said, I would have found you regardless." Crossing her arms over her chest, Grace grumbles something under her breath about men being infuriating.

Twenty minutes later, after she was done pouting, which is cute as fuck, Grace went on to tell me as much as she could about her husband. Now that I have an idea of what I am up against, it's time to get to the clubhouse and clue my brothers in on the situation.

Walking into the clubhouse, I see Gabriel, Logan, Reid, and Quinn. The four of them are sittin' at the bar. When they hear the door close behind me, all four sets of heads turn in my direction, and all four of my boys stand. Logan is the first to speak. "Everyone is in church." Lifting my chin, I stride across the room and down the hall with my boys at my back toward the room we hold church. When I walk in, I make my way to the head of the table. Once I slam the gavel, the men take their seats as I continue to stand as I have the floor.

"As you all know, Grace is back." At my statement, there is a collective round of fist pounding on the table and a few whistles, which causes me to chuckle because it feels damn good I finally have my woman. "Alright, alright, quiet down. Like I was saying, Grace is home, and by home, I mean she is at my place, which is now her place. Something else you all have already been clued in on is her daughter Remi. She is now with us too. Grace is mine. Therefore, Remi is mine. They both should be treated as such."

Squaring off and looking at each one of my men, they all give me a nod of understanding. "Now, with that out of the way, we're going to get down to business. I found out that Grace is married." I receive a few brow lifts from some of the men at my statement; my brothers are smart enough not to say a word so I continue. "Grace Cohen is Anna De Burca. She has been runnin' from her husband Ronan De Burca for over two years. Giving you the short version out of respect for my woman is, the motherfucker had been beating her for years, and the last time nearly killed her."

Once I deliver the blow, my men act like I knew they would. The room fills with anger and with the declaration of retribution. "You got any information on this guy?" This is coming from Reid.

"Yes, Grace has given me as much detail about him as she could, and I also spoke to O'Rourke before coming in today. O'Rourke has been investigating her husband and his family for a few years."

"What do you mean investigating?" Reid asks.

I pause a moment and gear myself up for the bomb I'm about to drop on the club. I wasn't prepared for what I learned this morning from O'Rourke. But if I know my brothers, they will not be deterred by the news. The Kings will not back down. My men will have my back.

"Grace said the De Burca family is very well-known and extremely powerful. She told me she's not sure as to what the family is into, but she is certain that whatever it is, it's illegal. Before she and Ronan were an item, Grace heard rumors about the De Burca family, but she was never brought into the happenings. So, I spoke to O'Rourke. He told me the De Burca are one of the most prominent Irish mob families in the Midwest. Dealing with drug trafficking, racketeering, and extortion. Not to mention the number of unsolved murders that surround the family due to lack of evidence."

I stop speaking for a moment to let what I just unloaded sink in. I don't miss several murmurs of *fuck* escape some of the men's mouths. "Shit with Grace just got real. O'Rourke said after he had Grace settled with her new identity and in a new town, he continued his investigation with the De Burca family. He's been in the wings watching and waiting for them to slip. But as you know, families like this with endless amounts of money and power at their disposal, O'Rourke is way out of his league. Grace admitted her mother tried to convince her while she and Ronan were dating to break things off and pleaded with her not to marry him, but Grace was in love, she wasn't going to see what other people saw."

"Then shortly after the two were married, Grace's mom's bakery was burned down, with her mom inside. The whole thing was ruled an accident. Supposedly a gas leak, but Grace always felt her husband was behind the fire. Her mother was constantly trying to convince Grace to leave Ronan. The only person Grace had in her life besides Ronan was her friend Glory. They grew up together. Glory lived in a different state, so Grace said she never got to visit her, but they called each other every week. She said she only mentioned Glory a handful of times to Ronan, and after things with her husband began to change, she kept her relationship with Glory a secret. Her friend was also not a big fan of Ronan, and with her suspicions of what she believed really happened to her mom, Grace was scared they would go after Glory."

"So, by this point, he had alienated her from her friends and taken care of the mother. And because Grace wanted to protect the only friend she had left, she was trapped. I'm also assuming she had her daughter by this time, which made her even more dependent on the motherfucker," Quinn interjects with anger in his voice.

Looking around the table at my brothers, they all are wearing a look of anger on their faces: no judgment or snide comments about how Grace could have been so naïve. I knew my brothers would give Grace nothing but love, support, and protection.

"What about the kid?" Gabriel asks. "This fucker put his hands on her?"

"No," I'm quick to answer. "Grace said she made sure her husband never touched Remi. My guess is she stepped in and took the punishments that were meant for her. She said as Remi got older, she learned how to stay out of her father's way. She learned the rules of the house and followed without protest. It's because of her daughter, Grace finally got the nerve to escape."

"What do you mean?" Logan inquires.

"Grace overheard her husband and his father talking. They wanted to start grooming Remi. At the time, she was only ten, but her marriage was already arranged. Remi was to marry the son of another prominent Irish family. The two were to join forces, and Remi was the ticket. She would be groomed and married as soon as she turned eighteen. Later, Grace confronted her husband, and that is when he beat her badly enough to land her in the hospital. That's when she met O'Rourke."

"Fuck, Prez. His own fuckin' kid?" Logan grits out as he lights a cigarette.

Pulling out my chair and sitting, I light a cigarette of my own and take a drag before I continue. "I didn't ask Grace for details. I don't think she's ready. It was hard enough to give me what she did. I will tell ya, that by my observation of Remi over the past couple of days is that the bastard has an old-school view of a woman's place in the home. I made the kid breakfast, and she sat at the table with her plate in front of her and wouldn't touch it. She was waiting and watching me. Like she wasn't allowed to eat until I did or some shit."

"Damn, Prez, that's fucked up," Quinn remarks.

"Yeah, it is, but I talked with her. I told her that's not how things work around here. She understands, but I'm sure it will take some time to break out of those old habits." We're all quiet for a few minutes absorbing the information I just handed. And when my eyes land on Reid, he's watching me intently. My brother already knows what's coming next. "I need you on this man."

"You got it, Prez." Reid nods.

"Thanks, son."

"In the meantime, I want you all to stay vigilant. Grace is home today with Remi, but if I know my woman, she's going to want to get back to doing what she loves, and that's the bakery." I turn my attention to Quinn. "I want you with Grace whenever I'm not. If she's at work, then that's where you are. I'm countin' on you, son. Can you handle this?"

"You know you can, Prez. Don't worry; I got Grace and Remi." With that, I slam the gavel down, ending church.

10

GRACE

Jake's place is beautiful and secluded, which I enjoy, but I'm starting to feel a little restless. It has nothing to do with being back or nerves. I'm feeling great now that I'm home with my daughter under the same roof as me. Now that I've given myself a few days to adjust to being back home and living in Jake's house for two days, all I can think about is getting back to work. I have lazed around and relaxed along with my daughter by my side. When Jake is not home, the two of us don't venture too far from the house. One, the fact is Ronan is still a threat to us and two, we don't know the area well. Jake lives so far out from town there happens to be a lot more wildlife we could run into like black bears.

Keeping his promise to Remi, Jake has taken her out the past two mornings to see his friend's horses, and in the evening the three of us have walked the property, because Jake is adamant we learn every square inch of it, and I agree.

I've talked with Glory every day since I've been back, and I'm feeling a bit uneasy about her being alone. Glory uprooted her life to help me. She's so close to her family, and for two years, she's kept little contact with them for us. I know her parents were supportive of the sacrifices she made, but it doesn't change the fact that she won't be able to go back home until Finn has the evidence he needs to put Ronan behind bars. Finn is good at keeping us informed, and the last we heard Ronan was still actively looking for me. In the beginning, Ronan and his goons harassed Glory's parents by grilling them on where his family was and accusing them of hiding us. In a way, they were. They didn't know where we went or where their daughter went but they knew part of the reason why. After they had a restraining order filed against him, Ronan resorted to having men stand outside across the street, sometimes for hours at a time watching her parents place until they finally moved on. I don't have my parents anymore, but I have Glory's mom and dad, and I would do anything to make sure they stay safe. They shouldn't have to suffer because of my poor choice in a man.

I'm enjoying a soothing cup of chamomile tea when Remi comes bounding down the stairs. "Mom, these clothes are awesome. Have you seen the stuff your friends picked out for me?" She beams. Jake thought the best way to introduce Remi to everyone, was all at once, and I agreed, so the club is having a cookout later today as a welcome home party for my daughter and me.

I love that she hasn't had any problems settling in since we got here. "I haven't, Bella and Alba will be happy to hear you like what they picked out. You can tell them in a few hours when you finally meet them," I remind her.

"I'm a little nervous," she climbs on the barstool beside me at the kitchen island and snatches a white chocolate macadamia nut cookie from the plate in front of her.

"Peanut, there is nothing to worry about. All of Jake's family are good people. Trust me; they'll love you," I try to reassure her while grabbing a cookie.

"Do I really have to go to work with you tomorrow?" she jumps straight into a new subject altogether while slumping her shoulders.

"Yes, and it's not open for discussion either, Remi," I remind her for the third time since yesterday. I know she wants to be a regular kid and go to school, but I don't think it would be possible. It's one thing for me to go around using a fake name to get by, but to enroll her in school, I would have to have more than a false photo ID. Having had enough mother-daughter time, she snatches another cookie from the plate and retreats upstairs to her bedroom.

A few hours later, Remi and I are buckled into Jake's truck and on our way to the clubhouse. Reaching over, I grab Jake's hand that's resting on the center console because touching him soothes me. When we arrive at the gate, a new guy I've never seen before lets us pass. "Haven't seen him before?" I comment.

"His name is Grey, he's a newbie lookin' to prospect for us," Jake explains, then pulls his truck alongside Bella's car. "Ready?" he asks as he turns off the ignition.

"Ready," I smile with confidence.

As soon as we step out of the truck, you can smell food cooking on the grill and kids laughing. The three of us proceed to walk through the front door of the clubhouse. I've never been out here or inside Jake's club before. The large room we walk into has a bar on one side, and a few pool tables, couches, and small round tables with chairs spread out amongst the room.

"This is the common room. It's where the guys hang out," Jake explains, then points to some stairs, "those go up to the second floor where the bedrooms are."

Remi being inquisitive, asks, "People live here?"

"Sometimes," Jake answers her.

"Cool," Remi remarks, causing a smile to appear on Jake's handsome face.

He walks us through a door that leads us into a kitchen where Lisa is standing at the stove, "Something sure is smelling good in here, woman," Jake's deep voice calls out, startling her.

"Jake," she looks over her shoulder. Noticing Remi and I standing beside him, she gasps, "Grace." She wipes her hands on a towel and lays it on the counter beside her before making her way toward me with her arms outstretched, "Welcome home," she hugs me, "and this must be Remi," she looks to my side.

"That's me," Remi tells her and holds her hand out.

"Oh, honey, this family likes to hug. Would it be okay if I hug you?" Lisa asks her permission. Bobbing her head, yes, both of them hug it out.

"Well, the rest of the gang is outside," Lisa warns. "The ladies have been chompin' at the bit, waiting for you two to get here," she adds.

I can imagine how they've been since I've been back home and stowed away out in the middle of nowhere. I'm thankful they understood Remi, and I needed a couple of days to breathe and root ourselves where we belong. I've missed their faces and friendships more than they will ever know. I grab Remi's hand, "No better way than to jump right in," I swing our arms and walk toward the sliding glass door, pull it open and step outside. No one spots us at first, which gives me a second to let my eyes sweep the yard. The first person to notice us is Bella. Her hand goes to her mouth, and she starts jogging across the yard. Bella and I became the best of friends over the two years I lived here. Despite what Bella has been through, she still chooses to see the positive aspects of life. Bella also knew I was falling for Jake, and yet she didn't meddle. Like Glory, she could read me and knew how much to hold back and when not to.

The closer Bella gets to me, my eyes zone in on the noticeable baby bump she is sporting. "Grace," she wraps me in a hug.

Embracing her, I blurt out, "Something you wanna tell me?"

Pulling back, Bella looks down at her little bump and rubs it, "We're expanding the family," she proclaims. "I'm so happy you're home, Grace." She hugs me one more time.

Before I can dive into further details with her, a crowd has gathered behind Bella's back.

"Wow, you have a big family, Jake," my daughter voices.

Refusing to let go of my hand, Bella looks at my daughter. "She looks so much like you, Grace," she gushes.

Jake steps up behind Remi and puts his hand onto her shoulders and faces everyone. "Everyone, this Spitfire is Remi." Jake looks down, "Remi," she tilts her head back, giving her attention to him, and he tells her, "**This is your family.**"

Consumed by the love standing around us, I lose it. Tears spill from my eyes with Jake's declaration to my daughter, claiming us in front of everyone. Alba joins her sister along with Mila, and even Emerson falls in beside her. Remi slips under my arm and wraps an arm around my waist, "You feel it?" she asks.

"I feel it, Peanut," I kiss the top of her head. *Love.*

YESTERDAY WAS AN EMOTIONAL DAY. Most of the day we spent with everyone catching me up on things I had missed. It's incredible how much I'd missed in the few months I was gone. Bella being pregnant is one of them. I watched her struggle along with the rest of her family and friends to start a family. Bella and Logan got to adopt the sweet baby she fell in love with while volunteering at the hospital, and they are now expecting a little boy. Watching all the little ones toddle around and play started to tug at my heart, and I started thinking about when Remi was a baby.

I also got to watch my daughter be carefree—be the kid she's supposed to be. Remi got along well with Sofia and ended up hanging with her most of the day, and I think her favorite club member is Quinn. It probably has something to do with the fact that they both have a quirky sense of humor, and she was keeping up with his little zingers, dishing them out as quickly as he was delivering them himself. All PG, of course.

It's early, just before sunrise, and my daughter and I are on the road heading toward town with Jake following behind us. Once we make it to the bakery, I park out front, and Jake pulls alongside me, turns his bike off, and dismounts. Remi and I climb out of my car, and the three of us walk to the front door.

"Let me know when you guys are ready for lunch, and I'll take my break with the two of you," Jake motions for me to hand him my keys, and he unlocks the storefront for me.

Stepping in first, he flips the overhead lights on and sweeps the room before letting us walk the rest of the way in. I find it comforting that he does the maneuver almost every time we enter any space. One of the things Jake insisted on before I came back to work was getting Reid to install a state of the art security system in and around the bakery. Previously, I only had the one camera inside, but now several small cameras are placed throughout. Now Jake can have access to live feed and check on Remi and me anytime he wants, but of course, he is still having one of the club members, Quinn as a matter of fact, hang around all day to help keep an eye on things. The good thing about the location of my store is I'm on the main street, which is a block from Kings Custom, so Jake won't be too far away.

Standing in front of the empty bakery glass windows, I reflect back to the first time Jake walked into the store. I had been open for almost a week at the time. A new town and all, I was nervous. It would be the first time I'd be running a place solo. I had spent the whole day before plus that night baking for my grand opening in the morning. I'm in an excellent location; next door is a clothing boutique, and on the other side is a small grocery store.

I'd been open for a couple of hours when Jake walked in with a menacing look on his face like someone had just messed up his morning. He had to have seen the look of worry on my face because his entire demeanor shifted, and his face softened. Jake quickly apologized for his grumpiness. It turns out he walked up on some guy giving a young lady a hard time near the alleyway of the grocery store, and he had just taken care of the situation before stepping through my doors that morning. He was stopping by to introduce himself, and said he liked to get to know everyone in town. My lips turn up in a smile as I slipped my apron over my head and secured the tie around my waist. Nearly every day after that one, he came in to buy doughnuts. He swore he and his guys couldn't get enough of them. He was either working out extra hard or fibbing because his fit physique never once showed signs that he was packing away that many calories.

"I see those wheels turning. What has you lost in thought, Little Bird?" Jake's voice rumbles, as he comes to stand in front of me and pushes my wild curls from my face.

"I was thinking about the ridiculous amount of doughnuts you've bought from me the past couple years," I tell him and slip my hand under the hem of his shirt, letting my palm skate across his abs.

Jake's large hand wraps around the base of my neck, causing me to lift my gaze from his chest and connect with his smoldering stare, "Kiss me, woman," he rasps before his mouth settles heavily over mine.

"See, this right here is one more reason I should be in school, a real school with other kids my age," Remi sighs.

Looking around Jake, I see her standing by the register with her arms crossed. "Peanut," I warn.

"Mom, come on, please. We passed the school on the way here, and it's close enough I could walk there. You need to focus on work, and I want to have friends. I can't make friends if I'm stuck in here with you all day. I want to be normal," she begs.

I feel bad. I know she hasn't had a normal life. And she's been homeschooled her whole life because of Ronan, but she needs to understand it's for her own good. It's so I can keep her safe. I don't know what else to do.

"If I could offer a solution, babe?" Jake interjects.

I rub my temples with the tips of my fingers, "I'm willing to hear what type of solution you could have," I tell him.

"Let me talk with Reid; maybe he can do for Remi what O'Rourke did for you. If I can find a way to keep her hidden and safe, would you consider letting her try school?" He rubs the sides of my arms as he speaks to me.

It's a huge risk. "If Reid can come up with all the required documents for Remi to be enrolled, then I will consider letting her go to public school," I state.

Hearing the rumble of a motorcycle draws our attention toward the window to see Quinn backing his bike alongside my car.

"If you need me, you call and put Quinn's ass to work doing something," Jake leans in to steal one more kiss.

11

JAKE

Riding down the main street behind Grace, I spot Quinn sittin' on his bike in front of the bakery smokin' a cigarette. Grace parks in her usual spot next to the alley as I pull in next to Quinn. Getting out of her car, Grace makes her way toward me while Remi jogs over to Quinn and begins chattin' with him. Remi has taken a shine to Quinn. Kids are drawn to him. He says it's his easy going and charming personality. I suppose it's because he acts like a big fuckin' kid all the time, and they see him as a peer. All the brothers give Quinn shit from time to time, but we wouldn't want him any other way.

I turn my attention back to my woman when she wraps her arms around my middle, and her scent invades my nostrils. "Will you be here at closing, or is Quinn following me home today?"

"I'll be here. I'm going to go see Reid, and we're going to find a solution for getting Remi in school." When I see apprehension flash across Grace's face, I tilt her chin up, forcing her to meet my eyes. "Whatever we come up with, I promise you your girl will be safe. The club won't let anything happen to Remi. I want you to trust me on this, Little Bird." Taking a shuttered breath, she runs her fingers through my beard, something I've come to love, and nods. "Yes, Jake, I trust you. It's just, Remi is my life. I'm always going to worry. But I know this is going to be good for her. I want her to have a normal childhood."

Kissing her on top of her head and then again on her lips, I murmur, "She will." Slapping her on the ass, "Now get inside. I'll see ya later." Turning on her heel in the direction of the bakery's front door, I watch the sway of her hips as she walks inside before I then turn my attention to Quinn, who is wearing a goofy-ass grin on his face. "What?" I gruff, narrowing my eyes.

"Nothin' Prez, just like seeing ya happy is all."

Losing some of the bite in my tone, I regard him, "Thanks, brother."

"Well, I'm going to get inside. My stomach is talkin', and Grace's cinnamon rolls are about to answer," Quinn says, getting off his bike and rubbing his hand over his stomach.

"Brother, you can't tell me Lisa didn't already feed your ass this mornin'. That woman doesn't let anyone leave the clubhouse without a full belly."

"Yeah, Prez, but that was two hours ago."

Chuckling, I shake my head, "Alright, man, I'm headed to see Reid. Call me if ya need anything."

"You got it, Prez," Quinn says, lifting his chin and then strides into the bakery.

With one last look at my woman through the window, I fire up my bike and head in the direction of Kings Construction.

Walking into Kings Construction, I see Leah sitting behind the front desk with her face hiding behind her glasses and mass of brown curly hair. Though Leah has been in Polson and around the club for over a year now, she is still shy as ever. I'm always mindful of my tone and how I approach her. The last thing I want to do is scare her. And this poor girl looks like she is scared of her own shadow. There's a story there for sure. I don't know much;

only she's layin' low from her father, and Nikolai and Reid pay her in cash.

"Hey, sweetheart, is Reid in yet?" I ask, striding up to the counter.

"Yes, Mr. Delane. Mr. Carter is in his office," she replies, her voice low.

"Thanks, sweetheart," I say, giving her a wink. "And no more of that Mr. Delane nonsense, okay? You can call me Jake."

With a slight blush, she drops her head and nods.

Walking down the hall, I stop in the doorway to Reid's office and see he is typing away on his computer. Rapping my knuckles on his door, I make my presence known.

"Hey brother, you have a minute?"

Peering up from his screen, "Yeah, Prez. Come on in." He gestures for me to take a seat in the chair in front of his desk. "You saved me a trip to the clubhouse. I was about to head that way." Reaching into his desk drawer, Reid pulls out a folder and hands it to me. "This is everything I found on Ronan De Burca."

"Excuse me," Nikolai cuts in from behind me. "My apologies, I don't mean to interrupt, but your door is open, and when I was walking by, I heard you mention the name Ronan De Burca?" I take in Nikolai's stature and notice his body language has gone tense.

"Do you know who Ronan is, son?" I ask.

Thinning his lips, Nikolai gives a tight nod. "Irish Mob," he states.

Knowing I can trust Nikolai, I state, "He's also Grace's husband." I watch as something like recognition passes over his face.

"Anna De Burca?"

Sitting up straighter in my seat, I turn to face him fully. "What do you know about Grace?"

"Personally? Nothing. The Volkov's have never worked with the

Irish. But that does not mean I don't know how they operate. Personally, I find their family unfavorable. The Volkov's are no saints, but my father and I refuse to work with any man who places such little value on their women. A few years ago, we heard rumors of Ronan and how his wife and daughter had disappeared. Some say she fled, and some suspected she was dead. Neither stories were surprising," he says, his voice dripping with malice. "Would you like mine and father's help? I'm going to assume The Kings are going to war if need be. The Volkov's will have your back," he declares.

"Make the call to Demetri. See when will be a good time for him to have a sit down with my brothers and me."

"I'll let you know something by days end," he confirms, offering me his hand, and I offer mine in return.

Once Nikolai has left, I turn my attention back to Reid. "As soon as I hear back from Volkov, I'm going to call church. Hopefully, with what information you dug up and whatever Demetri can tell us, we can get a better grip on what we are going up against."

"You got it, Prez," Reid backs me up without hesitation.

"Alright, in the meantime, I need your help with something else. Remi has voiced she wants to go back to school. Grace's friend Glory has been homeschooling her. Despite Grace's worries, she wants to make her daughter happy, and so do I. The kid is desperate for some normalcy and structure. I want to do my damndest to give her some."

"What did you have in mind, Prez?"

"Any way you can come up with a new name and a fake birth certificate, social security number? You know, all the shit kids need when registering for school?"

"I can do all that. No problem. I can have everything done in a few hours then drop it by the clubhouse."

"Thanks, son. I knew I could count on ya," I say, standing up.

"Listen, I know you guys have been swamped with the construction of the resort, but you think you can spare Austin? I want to put him on watch when Remi starts school. I'll want him wherever she is when she's not with Grace or me. If you can spare him, then maybe I can steal Blake away from Gabriel."

Reid shakes his head. "Nah Prez, you can have Austin. Sam is always willing to take on extra hours. He's a good kid and never complains. We'll make it work," Reid assures me.

"Alright, son. I'll see ya at the clubhouse in a bit," I tell him clapping him on the back.

Several hours later, I'm in my office back at the clubhouse when Logan comes striding in with Reid tailing him. Reid is the first to speak. "I have what you asked for Prez," he says, handing over a large manila envelope. It turns out, Montana has 176 girls between the ages of five and fifteen named Remi. So, I kept it simple. Remi De Burca is now Remi Cohen. I gave her the same last name as Grace."

"This is perfect. Thanks, brother," I say, but I am interrupted by Blake knocking on my office door.

"Prez, you have a visitor at the gate. Says his name is O'Rourke."

"What the hell is he doing back in Polson?" This is coming from Logan.

"Fuck if I know," I say, just as confused as I stand and make my way out of my office and toward the front of the clubhouse. "I talked to him the other day. He never mentioned anything about coming."

"He's got some balls showin' up at the clubhouse. Being a cop and all," Reid put his two cents in as he and Logan fall in behind me. And he's not wrong. A cop showin' up at our compound takes a fuck ton of guts. Damn, it's hard not to like this guy. Stepping out of the door and into the parking lot, I see Finn O'Rourke sliding out of his rented SUV. I also take notice of his appearance. The last time I saw him, he was in a suit that reeked of being a pig, but today he's in jeans, t-shirt, and boots. Finn being the man who helped my woman is what has earned him respect with my club. My brothers know about him, so cop or no cop, he will be treated accordingly. "O'Rourke, want to tell me what you're doing here?" I ask, crossing my arms over my chest. Leaning against his truck and casually crossing one foot over the other, he answers. "After our phone conversation a few days ago, I got the feeling that you and your men would soon be up to something."

"So, what? You thought you'd come to Polson and my clubhouse because you think you can stop us? Because I can tell you right fuckin' now, that shit's not happenin'," I challenge.

"I'm not here to stop you, Mr. Delane. I'm here to help."

I narrow my eyes with suspicion. "What the hell ya talkin' about?"

Pushing off the side of his SUV, O'Rourke comes to stand toe to toe with me. By this point, the rest of my men have joined us. Gabriel, Bennett, and Austin. We are all awaiting Finn's next words.

"I took a leave of absence from the force. I am not here as a cop. I'm here as Grace's friend and a friend of The Kings. I left my badge back in Chicago. Today I stand in front of you as a man who is ready to take on the De Burca family and put that son of a bitch, Ronan, in the ground," he finishes.

Leveling his stare for a moment, I determine I see nothing but the truth in his words. Holding my hand out to him, I ask, "You have a place to stay while you're in town?" Shaking my hand, he replies, "No. This was my first stop. But I was thinking of asking Grace if I could stay in her old place above the bakery."

I jerk my head toward the clubhouse, "You can follow me over there in a bit. She doesn't get off for another hour. In the meantime, let's go inside and grab a beer. And you can call me Jake. You showin' up here, puttin' your job on the line to help my woman; you've more than earned the right."

"I can handle that," he says, following me inside, "and thanks for not shooting my ass when I showed up."

Settling at the bar, I motion for Raine to give us a round of beers when I hear the door opening behind me. Turning in my stool, I watch Demetri and Nikolai walk in. "Heard, you may need a little help exterminating a De Burca infestation," Demetri says, leaning against the end of the bar. Raine, knowing what he likes, sets a tumbler of straight brown whiskey in front of him. "I would like the opportunity to be a part of this adventure," he smirks. The allure of violence gleams in his eyes.

"I'm out for blood—for retribution, brother. I plan on being Ronan De Burca's judge, jury, and his motherfuckin' executioner," I declare with a lift of my beer.

12

GRACE

With the last of the dishes loaded in the dishwasher, I slip my apron off and hang it on the hook next to the back door. My third full day at work, and it felt great. My first day at work had been spent with Remi and me baking. The very next day, I flip the closed sign around to open and so many people in town came by to say hello and let me know just how happy they were to see I was back. Of course, I had several ask why I left, but brushing it off as a family issue was more than enough to satisfy their eager curiosities.

Remi, however, has been on the edge of her seat ever since Jake said he would see what he could do about getting her enrolled in the local school down the road. I'm still a bit nervous about letting her go but know she needs it—she needs to feel and be a regular twelve-year-old girl. She has seen and been through far too much for her age as it is.

The only thing that puts my mind at ease is knowing Jake will do anything, and I mean anything, to make sure nothing happens to her.

When I walk to the front of the store, Remi has the broom in her hand as she finishes sweeping the floors. Without hesitation, Remi has always helped with chores.

She was born into what most would consider a privileged lifestyle, but I haven't raised her to think that way. I wasn't brought up with others picking up after me, and I plan on raising her the same way.

"Thanks for helping out, Peanut," I praise her while I begin to empty out the register and place the day's earnings in the lockbox in my office.

"Grace," Quinn walks out from the small break room, "Jake just called and said he'd be here in ten minutes. You got anything I can help with?"

"Sure, if you would grab the trash and throw it in the dumpster out in the alleyway, I need to put this money away and log it," I let him know as I place the cash into a bank bag, then zip it.

"You got it, pretty lady," Quinn responds before disappearing into the kitchen. Walking to the front door, I secure the lock, "Remi, come hang with me in the office until Jake gets here," I tell my daughter. She follows me into the office and sits on the edge of the small desk and swings her legs.

"Mom, do you think Aunt Glory would consider coming to live here or live with us?"

I ponder her question for a minute as I key in the numbers on the computer screen. It's not a bad idea. Polson is a pleasant town, and having her here would not only make Remi happy but me as well. "You know, I think we should ask her," I give an enthusiastic smile to my daughter. I watch the smile on her face fade and her brows furrow.

"Do you think we will ever stop hiding?"

The one question I have no answer for. Remi knows a lot but doesn't know the extent of the terrible person her father is, or the horrible things his family has done to people. She knows how abusive he is; she, unfortunately, witnessed his anger first hand on more than one occasion. No child should ever have to see or hear what she has seen and heard. She's also aware of the fact that her father and his family are suspected in the death of my mother— her grandma. My stomach sinks, and bile rises in my throat at the thought.

Ronan and his family have money; most of it blood money. It's one of the many reasons I've had to take on a different name and stay low key. "I hope so, Peanut. Finn is working very hard to put your father and as much of the De Burca family as he can behind bars."

Remi begins to draw a circle on the desktop with her fingertip, "I like it here. I love being with you. I really like your friends, and Jake's club is really cool. I don't ever want to leave here," she confesses with a low murmur.

"Me too," I agree. I'm done living under a rock. We've been given a second chance in life to have happiness, and I'm grabbing hold with both hands as tight as I can and not letting go.

Knuckles drumming on my office door takes my focus from Remi, and I turn my head and notice Quinn standing outside the open door.

"Jake just pulled up. I locked the back door, and everything else is shut down and secure for the evening. What do ya say we call it a day?" he tells me in his smooth and laid back tone. If only all of us could be that way. Quinn has a relaxed and easy-going attitude, and I have enjoyed being around him because of it. He has a way of putting Remi at ease. She talks a lot, and it doesn't seem to bother him. Quinn is a good man.

"Thank you, Quinn," I push my chair away from the desk and stand. "You ready to go home, Peanut?" I kiss her forehead, which earns me an eye roll with a smile. I'm very affectionate with my daughter. I always have been. I don't want her just to hear that she is loved. I want her to feel she is loved.

"Can we pick some pizza up tonight, and maybe a movie?" she

jumps down off the desk and walks to the far corner of my office to get her bag.

"Sure," I answer as we walk to the entrance of the store where Jake is waiting out front with Finn. *Wait a minute. Finn? Why would Finn be here?* Quinn unlocks the door, and the three of us walk outside to meet Jake and Finn on the sidewalk. "Come here, give me those lips, Little Bird," Jake's voice rumbles while my eyes continue to stay locked on Finn's, waiting for answers. Jake's hand snakes out and pulls me into his body. Tilting my head, I give him my full attention as his lips descend upon mine. My eyes close, and I melt into his touch, and I breathe in his smell of motor oil and grease cleaner he has acquired from working in the shop all day.

"You mind if Quinn takes Remi home?" his large calloused hand comes to rest on my face, and he uses the pad of his thumb to caress the apple of my cheek as he waits on my response.

"I get to ride on a motorcycle?" Remi squeals with excitement.

I turn to Quinn, "Please drive safe with her on the back of that thing," I tell him.

With his signature smile, he holds up his index finger, "First, my bike is not a thing she is a Harley Davidson Heritage Softail. Second," he holds up a second finger, "I've had my little sister on the back of my bike before, I can promise you I'll keep her safe, Grace."

Quinn has a little sister?

"Please, Mom," Remi grabs my hand and bounces. I look at Jake, and he smiles.

"Quinn may be a goof a lot of the time, babe, but I trust him," he says to put my mind at ease.

"Okay," I relent and turn to my daughter, "call me as soon as you get home," I inform her. Jake, Finn, and I watch as Quinn secures a helmet over her head and helps her onto the back of his bike. He slides his aviators over his eyes and signals a two-finger salute before pulling out and driving down the road. As soon as they are out of my sight, I fold my arms under my breasts and give Jake and Finn a look. "Alright, now someone let me in on what's going on," I ask the two of them.

Finn slips his hands into his pockets and is the first to speak. "Come on; I'm using the apartment above the bakery for a while. Let's head up, and we can fill you in," he ushers.

Eager to find out, I allow Jake to guide me up the stairs with his hand possessively placed on the small of my back. Jake reaches around me and unlocks my old apartment door. Everything inside is the way I left it. Dresser drawers left open in a rush and a couple of dirty dishes still sitting in the sink. The same wave of emotions I was feeling that night rush over me. I was scared to love someone again. Afraid of the feelings I had been hiding for a long time. I have let fear rule my life for a long time. Not anymore. "Okay," I place my bag on the kitchen counter, "I'm listening."

"I'm working with Jake and the club to bring down Ronan and several of his family members, and I've taken a leave of absence from the force to do it," Finn informs me.

"Wait. Why? What's changed? Has he found us?" I choked my words.

"No, babe," Jake assures me, "but O'Rourke feels The Kings can offer him something more. He's right; we can. We can offer him a reach that's beyond the law. The club has connections that can allow us more of a backdoor to the inner workings of the De Burca family. I know you are aware who Logan's father is, am I right?" Jake studies me.

Many conversations with Bella about her family have clued me into many facts, and my own experiences have made me acutely aware who Demetri Volkov is, or of him anyway.

"Anna...Shit, I'm sorry, Grace, I want you, Remi, Glory and her family to have a normal life again. I know that unless we put

Ronan behind bars or somewhere more permanent, that will never happen," Finn says with certainty.

He's right. The De Burca family is ruthless, and Ronan won't stop until he finds us. "Finn," I say with a sigh.

"Yeah?" he answers back.

"Two years. Ronan has been looking for us for two years. He took my mom from me; he almost took my life. The evidence you already have against him, you're positive it isn't enough to take them down?" I question. What the two of them are talking about puts all of us in the middle of a war zone. Should I have heeded the warning my parents gave me? Why did I have to be so blinded by what I thought was love?

"No, we need more to have anything that will hold up in court. Unfortunately, money talks and even dirty money if the amount is right can help persuade influential people. They have covered their tracks well, and we have found no witnesses to anything besides you. You are our only witness to a crime they have committed."

He's right. "Promise me one thing," I look to both of them, but my eyes settle on the man I love, "Promise me by the end of all this my daughter stays safe. I don't care about myself. The most important person in the middle of everything is Remi. It's always been Remi."

Jake takes my face in the palm of his hands, "Myself, the club, and O'Rourke will protect both of you with our lives, Little Bird. I can promise you that," he vows.

Standing a little taller, I hold back my emotions. I won't waste another tear due to the name Ronan De Burca or anyone associated with the last name. I'll fight alongside my new family if need be to protect the ones I love.

13

JAKE

It's early Sunday morning. Grace and I lay awake in bed with her tucked into my side. Both our internal clocks usually have us up before the sun. We lie here together, neither of us saying a word. Something Grace and I have in common is that we are content with silence. Although this morning, she is the first to break the stillness. "Will you tell me about your wife?" Rolling over Grace turns to face me, then tucks her hands under the side of her face as her eyes fixate on mine. "You've told me she passed away from cancer, but you have never really talked about her." Gauging Grace's face, I see nothing but warmth and curiosity, and she must take my silence for something else because she tries to shut down her question. "Never mind. I shouldn't have asked. I'm sure this is a painful subject for you," she rushes out as she goes to move away from me.

Reaching out, I snag her around her waist and haul her back toward me. "Come here, babe," I rumble. "You have nothin' to be sorry for. I want you to know you can ask me anything." Once her body relaxes back into me, I continue. "I never talked about Lily because I wasn't sure if you wanted to hear about her."

"Of course, I want to hear about her," Grace says. "I just never asked because she was your wife. Losing someone is painful. I still have a hard time talking about my mom and dad. So, I can't begin to imagine the pain of losing a spouse. I'm so sorry you had to go through that, Jake," she chokes out.

"Don't cry for me, Little Bird," I say, claiming her mouth with mine. After stealing a kiss, I sit up on the bed and lean back against the headboard bringing Grace with me, and she rests her head on my chest and wraps her arm around my waist. "I only had Lily a few short years, but I'll always cherish the time I had with her.

Lily was spontaneous, quick-witted, caring, and at times wild. I met her not long after I retired from the Army. She came into the garage one day, and the rest is history. We fell in love, married, and she was by my side when I started the club, and I was by her side when her sister died, and we took Logan in.

Then I was by her side when she was diagnosed with cervical cancer, and then I held her as she took her last breath. When Lily died, I thought she took a part of me with her. I was lost for a long time. Until you."

Feeling wetness spilling onto my chest, I look down to find Grace silently crying. Placing my finger under her chin, I coax her to look at me. "The first day I walked into your bakery, and you looked at me, that was the day I was found. That was the day I no longer felt I was roaming around this earth without a purpose because, in that exact moment, I had found my purpose. Before Lily died, she made me promise that when I found the woman I knew was meant to be mine, to never let her go. You, Little Bird, are my promise. Nothing and no one on this earth is going to take you from me," I say with conviction.

By the time I'm done speaking, Grace has tears running down her face, and I wrap my arms around her and haul her up my body and hold her as she buries her face in my neck. Once her tears have stopped, and her body is no longer trembling, Grace pulls her face from my neck and cups my face with her delicate hands. "I love you, Jake Delane."

"I love you too, babe," I say, kissing each of her tear-streaked cheeks before claiming her mouth with mine.

An hour later, Grace, Remi and I are in my truck as we cruise down the road. I told the girls we were going out for breakfast. When we make our way down a long paved driveway and park in front of a two-story colonial-style home, Grace asks, "Where are we? I thought you said we were going out for breakfast."

"We are. Ma cooks breakfast every Sunday," I say, shutting down the truck and stepping out before Grace has a chance to say anything back. When I walk around to the passenger side door and open it, I am not at all surprised to see a furious looking Grace.

"I can't believe you brought me to meet your parents without telling me," she fumes, crossing her arms over her chest while not attempting to get out of the truck. In the meantime, Remi wastes no time flinging her door open and rushing over to the field about thirty yards to my right. Grace immediately jumps in her seat and darts her eyes over my shoulder to see where Remi is headed. "She's going to see the horses, babe. She's safe out here," I assure her with a soft tone.

Relaxing her posture, I step forward into the truck and snake my arms around her middle and scoot her body around to face me. Leaning in, I rest my forehead against hers. "I didn't tell you because I knew you would be nervous and work yourself into a frenzy. My parents have wanted to meet you for two years, babe." At my confession, Grace's eyes go round. "Two years," she squeaks.

"Yeah, babe. My parents know about you. They knew about you since the first week we met. They're even excited to meet Remi. Ma has been chompin' at the bit. She likes havin' someone to spoil," I chuckle. "What do you say, babe? Want to meet my folks?" I ask, nudging her side, and my action earns me the sweet sound of her giggle.

Nodding, she says, "Yeah, I want to meet them. I'm sorry I got so worked up."

"You have nothin' to be sorry about, babe," I remind her again as I offer her my hand to help her step down out of the truck.

No sooner do I shut the door when my mother steps out of the house and onto the front porch, followed by my dad, both wearing big ass smiles. By the time we make it to the front steps, Remi runs up behind us and stands at her mom's side.

Before I have a chance to make introductions, my mother beats me to it by pulling Grace in for a hug. "It's so good to finally meet you, Grace."

Returning her embrace, Grace replies, "It's nice to meet you too, Mrs. Delane."

"Oh, honey, you can call me Karen. And this is my husband, Charles." Once their introductions are over, my mother's attention turns to Remi. "And who is this beautiful young lady?"

"Ma, this is Grace's daughter Remi."

With a warm smile, my father speaks up. "I saw you over with the horses. Would you like to ride one sometime?" he asks.

"Yes!" she shouts with excitement. And just like that, my father has won Remi over. "Alright," my father chuckles. "How about we eat some breakfast, and if it's okay with your momma, we'll go for a ride."

Remi turns to Grace. "Can I, Mom?"

"Sure you can, as long as it's no trouble."

"Oh, it's no trouble at all."

An hour and a half later, after breakfast, Grace insisted on helping Ma with the dishes, and now the three of us are sitting on the porch watching my dad teach Remi how to saddle a horse. When I cut my eyes to Grace, she is beaming from ear to ear as she watches her daughter.

Over the next couple of hours, conversation flows as Ma asks how all the boys are doing and how excited she is that Logan and Bella are expecting. My parents love Logan and think of him as their grandson. They have pretty much taken on the grandparent role with all the guys. As the afternoon wears on, we say our goodbyes to my parents, and my mom hands me a foiled covered plate. "For Quinn," she tells me, and I smile and shake my head.

With a promise to come back next Sunday, we load up and head in the direction of the clubhouse. "Are you cool with hangin' at the clubhouse for a bit. The guys and I have church, and I think all the women are there. Bennett said something yesterday about Lisa getting everyone together for dinner. But if you're not feelin' up to it, I can take you home."

"No, I think dinner with everyone sounds nice," she says, threading her hand through mine, and I lift them, kissing the back of hers. When we pull up and park in front of the clubhouse Remi once again jumps out and runs inside, no doubt seeking out the children. I'm thrilled she has adapted and embraced the club and my family.

Inside, Grace and I are met by my brothers, O'Rourke, Nikolai, and Demetri sitting at the bar and Ember serving drinks. As soon as Quinn notices us, he stands from his perch and strides in our direction. He wastes no time taking the dish my mother gave me out of my hand, then mumbles a quick thanks before heading off in the direction of the room we hold church. I watch as all the other men follow suit.

I turn to Grace. "Are you going to be okay while I talk with the guys?"

"I'll go see what the girls are up to in the kitchen. I promise I'll be fine. Now go and quit worrying about me."

Going up to her tiptoes, Grace kisses me before turning and making her way to the kitchen, and I head in the direction of the room church is held in. Walking into the room, I cut my eyes around and note that everyone is here before closing the door and striding around the table to my seat. Slamming the gavel, I direct my first question to Demetri. "I want you to tell me everything you know about the De Burca family."

"The De Burcas' are the second most powerful Irish family in the Midwest. Last I heard they were looking to join forces with the Curran family who is the number one most powerful Irish family. They live in Boston. Once the two families unite, they will hold a great deal of power and essentially become the most powerful syndicate in this country," Demetri explains without sugar-coating his words.

"Fuck me," I hear Logan from my right. Demetri's words even have Quinn's attention as he stops eating.

"What's the plan, Prez?" This is coming from Gabriel, who has remained silent throughout the meeting.

"It's time to prepare for war," I say without missing a beat. "It's time for my woman to stop hidin' and start livin'. She and Remi will never be able to do so unless Ronan is in the ground, and that's where I plan on puttin' the motherfucker."

"Do you require my assistance, Jake?" Demetri asks.

"I hate to ask you to put yourself in my shit show, but I'm not stupid enough to turn down your offer. Any assistance you can provide would be appreciated, brother."

"This club is my son's family. Therefore you all are my family. The Volkov's will stand with you." At his father's declaration, Logan sits up straighter in his seat and gives his dad a nod.

"We're runnin' low on artillery, Prez," Quinn cuts in. "The warehouse is damn near empty. Been that way since we quit runnin' guns."

"Weapons won't be a problem," Demetri adds. "Give me a list of what you need, and I can have it here in a week, maybe two. I'll have several of my best men accompany the shipment."

"Sounds good. Quinn, I want you to get with Demetri on what we need."

"You got it, Prez," he nods.

I cut my attention back to Logan. "I want you to put a call into Riggs. See how things are goin' down South. If all is quiet, ask him to be on standby. We might require his assistance."

"On it," he replies.

I'm just about to wrap the meeting up and bring church to an end when there is a knock on the door, followed by Lisa's voice. That gets everyone's attention. The woman knows we are not to be interrupted during church unless necessary.

Bennett is out of his chair and opening the door within seconds, and we can see she is visibly upset. "I'm sorry to interrupt, Jake, but you need to get Grace," she pleads, her voice shaky.

I am up and out of my seat before the word Grace finishes leaving her mouth. I'm storming down the hall with my men hot on my heels when I hear a frantic Grace. Rounding the corner of the kitchen, I'm almost brought to my knees with what I see in front of me.

Grace is on the floor, hunched over and rocking back and forth on her knees with her face buried in her hands sobbing. Ignoring everyone around us, I stride to my woman, lean down to one knee, and scoop her shivering body into my arms. Grace complies while fisting my shirt and tightly clings to me as she hides her face in my chest. "Lisa, come with me," I bark walking out of the kitchen, pass the bar and upstairs to my room.

When we get to my door, I motion for Lisa to open it. Walking ahead of me, she turns the lamp sitting on the table by the bed on as I lay Grace down on the bed. "I'll be right back, Little Bird. Can Lisa stay with you for a minute?" Releasing her hold on me, Grace nods, and I kiss her temple.

"I want you to stay with Grace," I tell Lisa. "Lock this door, and nobody but me can enter."

"No problem," she says without complaint as she goes to sit on the bed beside Grace and begins to stroke her back. This is one of the many things I love about Lisa. She is quick to take care of those she loves. "Thanks, sweetheart," I say, kissing the top of her head.

Returning to the kitchen, I see Bella, Alba, and Mila visibly shaken by the events that transpired here moments ago. I also see Ember cleaning a shattered bowl and mashed potatoes off the floor, and to my left, I see a very angry looking Raine shooting daggers at Liz.

I don't even know why the hell that bitch is here. The women love Ember and Raine, but Liz isn't usually welcome around Old Ladies. "Who wants to tell me what the hell just happened here?" I ask my voice hard.

Bella is the first to speak up. "One minute we were all chattin' and about to set the table and the next I hear a loud crash and Grace is on the floor frantically trying to clean the mess while pleading with us not to punish her. I think she was having a flashback." By the time Bella finished her account of what happened, she turns into Logan upset.

Fuck.

I'm about to turn and leave the room when I pause as Raine speaks. "That's not all that happened."

"Explain," I demand.

Without taking her eyes off Liz, Raine pushes off of the counter and steps in front of Liz. "This bitch," she says, pointing her finger at Liz, "shoved Grace with her shoulder, causing her to drop the bowl. I heard her tell Grace, '*Look what you did. What the fuck is wrong with you?*'" Taking another step closer to Liz, Raine gets right in her face. "Yeah, you didn't think I saw that shit, but I did."

"I don't know what the fuck you're talking about. I didn't do shit," Liz counters.

Without a second thought, I rush to Liz, grab her by the arm, and press her against the wall. "You made the wrong fuckin' move messin' with my woman," I spit.

"That bitch is lying," Liz tries pleading once again.

"Shut the fuck up!" I bellow in her face. "I know she isn't lyin'. You, on the other hand, have been deceiving this club for too long. You are no longer allowed on Kings' property. When you walk your ass out of my club tonight, you better be thankin' God I decided not to put a bullet between your eyes. Because woman or not, fuckin' with what's mine will get you dead. Do I make myself clear?"

Once Liz sees, I mean every fuckin' word I just delivered, she nods.

"Gabriel!" I bark over my shoulder. "Get this whore out of my club. She has ten minutes to pack her shit."

"You got it, Prez," Gabriel says snaggin' Liz by the arm and leading her out of the kitchen.

Looking around the room at the rest of my men, I give them a nod, silently telling them the show is over and for them to take their women home. A few seconds later, the kitchen has cleared all except for Ember and Raine, who are busy cleaning the mess. Walking over to Raine, I place my hand on her shoulder giving it a light squeeze. "Thank you, sweetheart. You did good tonight. You proved your loyalty to the club and my woman. You have my respect."

"You're welcome, Jake. Go on and see to Grace. She needs you. Ember and I got this."

Leveling both girls with one more look, I turn on my heel and head upstairs to Grace. On the way there, I pass Logan, Bella, Sofia, and Remi. "Is it okay if Remi stays with us tonight?" Bella asks. "She and Sofia talked about having a movie night. You think Grace would mind?"

I run my hand down my face, "I think Remi stayin' with you guys would be a great idea. I'm sure Grace won't mind."

"Yay! Thank you so much, Jake," Remi cheers, then steps forward and wraps her arms around my waist, hugging me. It is not lost on me that this is the second time she has embraced me. I note that this is a big step for her. It shows she is starting to open up and trust me. Returning her hug, I ruffle the mass of red curly hair on her head. "I want you to be good. I'll have your momma call you before bed, okay."

"Okay, and I'll be good. I promise."

Walking into my room, Lisa is sitting in a chair by the bed, and Grace is fast asleep. Without a word, I lean over and lift her into my arms. "Jake," she murmurs.

"Shhh, it's okay, baby. I'm going to take you home."

"Remi?"

"She's staying with Logan and Bella tonight. No worries, baby, she's safe," I say, walking out of the clubhouse and to my truck. Opening the passenger side door, I sit Grace down and buckle her in.

"I'm so embarrassed," Grace confesses as she looks at me with her tear-stained face and red puffy eyes.

"You have nothin' to be embarrassed about, Little Bird," I say, resting my forehead on hers. "My family is now your family, and they love you. Not one of them would ever judge you for what happened tonight. If anyone can understand demons, it's them. Every one of us has had to face down our own demons a time or two. Just remember your family will be there to help you through."

14

GRACE

"I've never had that happen to me before. It was like having one of my nightmares, but I was awake, yet out of my body at the same time." Holding my arms around my waist, I take in a breath to steady the beating of my heart. It was like I was right there. The images are so vivid; if I reached for them, I could grasp them.

"Babe, listen to me, you had a flashback. Many people who have been through trauma in their life suffer from them. It can sometimes be associated with PTSD. Maybe you should look into seeing someone about it."

Maybe Jake is right. Perhaps I need to talk with someone. I think therapy might be something both Remi and I could benefit from.

"Talk to me, Grace. Tell me where you were after dropping the bowl on the floor," Jake urges.

Releasing a thick, heavy sigh, I stare at my lap and wring my hands together. "Ronan wouldn't tolerate anything less than perfect, and that included me. Over time berating me for little things like a dirty glass in the sink or toys on the floor turned into more. You've seen the marks on my back," I pause and close my eyes.

"Shit," Jake mutters.

"We had guests over one evening. Some judge, I can't remember his name. Ronan had been on edge the whole day because this dinner was important to him. Like always, I was in the kitchen cooking dinner while Remi was upstairs in her room. I think she was nine at the time, anyway, I dropped a large platter holding the rack of lamb. I knew it was coming. He flew into the kitchen so quick I didn't have much time to react. I was frantically trying to pick up the mess before he started in on me. With company on the way, I didn't think he would do much more than raise his voice, but that wasn't the case. In a flash, his belt came off, and as I hunched over, the first strike of the leather strap made contact." Lifting my head, I glance at Jake's face expecting to see pity. I don't know why I was waiting for him to look at me that way. He wasn't. He never has. Jake has a determined look in his eyes.

"You may not know it yet, Little Bird, but you are a fiercely strong woman. You've been through the kind of hell no woman or person should have to go through, especially by the hands of someone claiming to love you. You survived. I have so much respect and admiration for you, Grace. Don't ever think or let anyone ever make you feel or tell you different. That son of a bitch sealed his fate the moment he put his hands on you, I promise you." By the time Jake finishes, I've calmed down.

The rest of the night feels like it has gone to shit. Wanting nothing more than to go home, I let Jake know, "Take me home. The only therapy I need tonight is you."

A FEW DAYS HAVE PASSED, and Remi gets to start her first day of public school today, and I believe I heard her in the kitchen earlier not long after Jake went downstairs to make coffee. I've been lying here for the past thirty-five minutes listening to the two of them go on about his parent's horses and Jake's little talk about strangers. It was his brief mention of boys that had me in a fit of giggles now.

Throwing the blanket off my body, I swing my legs over the edge of the bed. After making a trip to the bathroom and getting myself ready for the day, I head downstairs toward the kitchen to join Jake and my daughter. I find them sitting at the table, eating breakfast.

"Good morning," I kiss the top of Remi's head once I've reached the table. Jake stands and pulls me into him.

"Go ahead and sit down. I'll bring you some coffee and a plate of food." Leaning into one another, we share a kiss. It's still a little odd to have someone who loves to dote on me as Jake does.

Taking a seat across from Remi, I take a moment to stare at her. She went through several outfits and hairstyles to wear on her first day of school over the past couple of days. I even allowed her to buy some makeup as long as she kept her look natural. Like me, her style is simple. A pair of burgundy jeans paired with a white shirt, navy blue hoodie, and black converse on her feet. She has managed to tame her wild red curls by braiding her hair into a fishtail braid, which drapes over her left shoulder—the braided style she spent hours learning how to do.

"Mom, what's wrong? Why are you looking at me like that? Do I look okay?" Remi worries, immediately looking down at herself.

"No, Peanut, there is nothing wrong with you or your clothes. You look beautiful, as always. It's hard to see you growing up so fast, that's all," I tell her with a smile.

Nervously twirling her hair, she remarks, "I'm so excited to go to a public school, but I'm a little nervous about being the new kid. What if no one talks to me?"

Jake saunters over to the table and sits my plate filled with scrambled eggs, jelly toast, and two pieces of bacon in front of me along with a mug of coffee. Lifting the cup, I take a sip enjoying the warmth.

"You won't have a problem making friends, sweetheart," Jake says before I get the chance to say it myself. "And if there happens to be that one dumbass who has a problem with you, then fuck them. Don't ever let someone make you think they are better than you. No one will ever be better than you," he finishes and pops the last piece of bacon on his plate into his mouth.

Watching Remi's reaction to Jake's words makes my day. Her smile reaches her eyes in one big expressive emotion. To have someone, a man in our lives, to care so much to love her so much is overwhelming. Jake's love and devotion are fierce. It reminds me of how my papa was with my mom.

Looking at the time, I take a few bites of my breakfast, and down the rest of my coffee. "We need to get going. I have a meeting with the principal this morning, and we don't want you to be late on your first day." After gathering our things, Remi and I load up in the car while Jake locks the door before getting on his bike to follow us to town.

As promised, Austin is sitting outside the school in the parking lot across the street. He and Grey will take shifts throughout the day to keep an eye on things. Technically, we are testing the waters on this whole idea. I want it to work for Remi's sake because she wants normalcy in her life so bad, as do I. The threat of her father, however, is still a shadow over our heads.

Parking the car, my daughter and I make our way inside while Jake stops by the large black SUV Austin is keeping watch in. Standing, with my hand on the entrance to the school, I turn to Remi. "You ready?"

Hoisting her bag to her shoulder, she says, "Ready."

Once we make it through the two secured doors and into the office, Remi and I have a brief conversation with the school counselor before she introduces her to Sarah, the office helper for the day who looks to be around the same age as Remi. I was hoping for a least a hug goodbye but instead got a quick wave and a smile over her shoulder as she walked away and quickly got lost in girl chat with Sarah, who was tasked with taking Remi to her homeroom class. I felt a sudden ache in my heart watching her disappear around the corner, but it subsided as soon as I heard her laughter echo off the stone walls accompanied by the other girl's giggles. *She's got this.*

"Ms. Cohen, Mr. Kelly is ready for you," the counselor, Mrs. Sullivan, addresses, and points to the right of me toward a door, "no need to knock," she adds with a smile.

Pushing the door open, I find a middle-aged man sitting behind a desk, stirring a cup of coffee. He looks up from the paper in his hands, "Ms. Cohen, how are you this morning? Would you like a cup?" he gestures, holding up his mug.

"I'm okay, and thank you for the offer, but I'll pass on the coffee," I tell him and take a seat in the chair across from him.

He clears his throat, "I've been made aware by your lawyer of the custody matter at hand and that your ex-husband is not to have any contact with..." he looks down at the paper in front of him, "Remi."

Lawyer? I do my best to keep my face neutral though I'm very confused by his statement.

"I can assure you that we will take great care and exercise extreme caution with her safety. I've also talked with your fiancé, Mr. Delane." I raise my brow and lean back against the back of the chair while he continues to talk. "Jake's a good guy. I've known him for several years now. He keeps my touring bike in top condition."

"Well, Mr. Kelly, I feel a little better knowing you and the staff have been made aware of my current situation. We are hoping Polson will be a good place for my daughter to finish her schooling." I play along as best I can to the storyline Reid and Jake hatched. I honestly do feel better knowing they will be more alert to her wellbeing and safety. Jake seems to know everyone in town and has a lot of respect from them as well.

"You have nothing to worry about, and may I also say welcome back. Your bakery was closed for awhile, and I missed those wonderful double chocolate chunk cookies my wife would bring me every week." He leans forward, "She tried her best to create them. Not that they weren't good. They just weren't yours. I don't know what you put in them, but those cookies are addictive," he leans back and pats his stomach.

"It's good to be back and send your wife to the bakery; I'll send her home with a fresh batch tomorrow. As a thank you for understanding and helping keep my daughter safe," I tell him.

"I look forward to it. Once again, Ms. Cohen, rest assured, your daughter will be fine." He stands, and I do the same as we end the meeting. Mr. Kelly walks me out of his office. I thank him one more time before leaving.

Jake is waiting by my car, kicked back on his bike. Deserving a kiss, I walk straight to him, and a light tug on his beard brings his lips to mine. "Thank you for making sure she stays safe," I say, between pressing my lips to his a few more times.

"No thanks needed, Little Bird. Let's get to work before I decide to take you home and keep you to myself for the day," he states.

A FEW HOURS LATER, as I am putting out a batch of fresh double stuffed cookies, the front door chimes. Peering through the glass case, I watch Bella and Emerson walk in, and Bella has Breanna in her arms.

"Hey girl, how are you doing today?" Bella walks to the counter and waits for me to reply.

"I'm better. Sorry about the other night, guys. I didn't mean to ruin the evening," I admit.

"You didn't ruin a thing. The important thing is you are okay,"

Bella tells me as I close the display case and walk around the counter to greedily take Breanna from her arms.

"You know who puts a smile on my face? This little girl right here," I snuggle Bella's daughter in my embrace. "I missed the moments when Remi was this little with little cherub cheeks, and full of innocence," I express as I inhale the soft smell of baby shampoo from her hair.

"So, the other reason we came by was to tell you a new kickboxing class opened over by the gym, and the instructor is offering self-defense classes. Bella and I were thinking about checking the place out later and wanted to know if you might want to join us," Emerson adds as she walks over to the cookie samples and lifts the lid grabbing one.

"Yeah, I've talked about taking some classes like this for a long time now, and Logan thinks it's a great idea. The doctor cleared me," Bella rubs her small baby bump. "And I know Alba wants to check it out too," she adds.

"Sure, I can close a little early today. I want to be the one to pick Remi up from school anyway. I'm anxious to hear how her first day went." Handing Bree back to her mommy, I retrieve my phone from my pocket and shoot a text to Jake, letting him know of my plans.

Jake: Closing early to pick up Remi. Taking her with me to spend time with the girls.

It doesn't take long for him to respond.

Me: Alright, babe. Take Quinn.

"Where's Quinn?" asks Emerson looking around the store.

Wearing a smile, I tell her, "Jake wants me to put him to work while he watches over me, so he has kitchen duties now that

Remi is in school, and I don't have her helping out. It would go a lot quicker, but my dishwasher went out this morning in the middle of the wash cycle, so everything needs to be cleaned by hand."

"I bet that burns his ass." Emerson giggles with amusement.

"Not really. He's so laid back. I don't think there is anything I could ask of him that would make the man mad. Besides, Quinn sings when he works, and he has a nice voice." As soon as I say that, Emerson perks up. "He sings?"

"Yeah, I haven't let him on to the fact that I listen in on him. He only does it when he's alone or when he's helping Remi in the kitchen, but he's pretty good," I tell her. I check the time. I've got about forty minutes before I close up for the day and head to the school to pick my daughter up. "How about I meet you guys there. If this place is by the gym, then I won't have any problems finding it."

"Great," Bella sings. "Oh, and don't worry about workout clothes. I need to stop by the house and drop Bree off. Sofia offered to watch her for an hour. I should have something you can use."

"Sounds good. It saves me a long trip out to Jake's and back. So, I'll see you guys in an hour?" I ask to make sure I won't be late.

With all the baked goods stored until tomorrow, I flip the open sign to closed and head to my car while Quinn locks the door.

"You going home after picking Remi up, darlin'?" Quinn inquires as he swings a leg over his bike.

"I'm meeting Bella and Emerson at a new boxing studio that opened next to the gym. The instructor is holding self-defense classes, and they asked if I wanted to join them." Pushing the button on my key lock, I unlock my car door and swing it open.

"Emerson will be there?" he asks. Nodding my head, I confirm what I said with a knowing smile. "Aw hell. This I got to see. Lead the way, darlin'. You just made my fuckin' day," Quinn proclaims as he pulls his shades over his eyes and secures his helmet on his head.

I wait outside the school in the car rider lane for about ten minutes when the bell finally rings. Eagerly I scan the sea of kids milling out of the school doors until I spot my daughter's red hair amongst all the heads. She's walking with the same young girl who escorted her to class this morning, and she's wearing a massive smile on her face. I can't wait to hear about her day. Waving goodbye to her new friend, she opens the door and sinks into the passenger seat and chunks her bag between her feet.

"Mom, I had the best day," she beams, closing the door and buckling in. "I've been asked if I want to join the cheer squad," she claps her hands in excitement.

"That's great, Peanut."

"Thanks, Mom," she adds as we follow the line of cars out of the parking lot.

"For what, sweetie?"

"Letting me go to school and being home with you. I'm happy, that's all," she shrugs her shoulders as to say it's no big deal. *It's a big deal. My baby is happy.*

"Bella and Emerson have invited me to take a self-defense class this afternoon. If you have any homework, you can tune us out by working on it at the gym," I inform her as I drive down the road.

"And miss you kick some butt. No way. And I don't have any homework. I did it in class. It was super easy."

The girls don't know Finn taught me self-defense right after I disappeared. He teaches all the women he helps to defend themselves. I haven't practiced in a long time, though, so I'm hoping I haven't forgotten anything. Noticing Bella's car, I park next to her, and we climb out. Quinn backs in on the other side.

"Hey, Quinn," Remi waves.

"Hey there, shorty. How was your first day? Do I need to kick any shitheads in the balls?" he smirks, causing Remi to giggle.

"No. The boy who talked to me was nice," she tells him then quickly tries to disappear through the gym door, but not before Quinn has something to say.

"Oooh, I'm telling Jake you talked to boys," he picks at her and laughs.

Leaving Quinn, I join my daughter inside, where she has already found Bella and Alba standing near the back by some lockers. Waving me over, I wind my way around floor mats laid out across the floor.

"Here. You can use the bathroom behind us to change. The instructor should be out in a few minutes, and Emerson will be showing up in a minute, too," Bella says, handing me a pair of workout shorts, sports bra, and a tank.

Retreating to the bathroom, I change. When I emerge with my other clothes in hand, Bella takes them and places them in a locker where her things are located. Quinn walks in, scanning the room until spotting us and strides over.

"Prez said he'd be here in thirty minutes to wait and follow you home," he informs me. Just then, Emerson opens the gym door and walks inside.

"Jesus Fuckin' Christ," Quinn mutters as our eyes follow his across the room. Emerson is a beautiful woman. It's not often anyone sees her not wearing her scrubs. Her tattoos are sexy. She has a beautifully detailed peacock tattoo that starts at her ribcage, and the feathers span her hip and partly down her thigh. It's breathtaking. It's on full display with her gym outfit.

"Who the fuck is that douchebag?" Quinn points and glares.

My eyes follow the direction of his finger. The guy he is referring to is speaking to Emerson and making her laugh, which I'm positive Quinn won't tolerate for too much longer judging by the scowl on his face.

"That's Rhett, the instructor. We met him earlier today when we signed up," Bella announces with her arms above her head as she puts her long hair into a ponytail.

"Alright, ladies. My name is Rhett. Let me begin by saying this is a safe environment. Learning to defend yourself against an attacker can be an overwhelming thought for some, but trust me when I say you are stronger than you think you are. Now, Emerson here," he motions for her to walk on the mat, "just started taking Muay Thai classes last week. She has agreed to help me show you a few moves to get us started."

"I'm not sure I can watch another man touch my woman like this," Quinn runs his hand through his shaggy blonde hair before shoving them both in his front pockets. Emerson takes her stance. The instructor is demonstrating how to get out of a hold if an attacker should grab her by the arm. He teaches how to twist the elbow upward, yanking downward using our core muscles, then fleeing. Next is a simple grab from behind and lifted off the ground move. He instructs her to use the heels of her feet to kick the shins of the attacker repeatedly.

Feeling good about herself so far, Emerson smiles when Rhett praises her, "Perfect. Ladies, that was a great example of how to make these two moves." Motioning for her to leave the mat, Emerson saunters toward us. Holding our breath, we wait for Quinn to say something, but he doesn't. Instead, he makes his way over to the side of the room where Remi is watching, but not before he makes sure Emerson sees his eyes lustfully roam her body, which causes her to blush. When the two of them, or I should say whenever Emerson decides to give in to the chemistry the two of them have, anyone within a hundred mile radius will feel its effect; it's that intense already.

"So, which one of you ladies is willing to help demonstrate a few more moves," the instructor asks.

Feeling brave, I raise my hand, and it takes my friends off guard. I know this by the shocked looks on their speechless faces.

As I step my foot on the mat, the sound of the front door closing catches my attention, and I find Jake standing there. Our eyes connect, and butterflies flutter in my stomach with his heated stare.

The instructor clearing his throat grabs my attention. When I turn my head, giving him my attention, he provides a quick glance to Jake. I give him a shoulder shrug and smile before introducing myself. "Hi, My name's Grace," I tell him and wipe my sweaty palms on my hips. *You've got this.* I say to myself and focus.

"Grace, nice to meet you. Class this is Grace, she's going to help me demonstrate two more defensive moves," he announces and instructs me to face forward and that he is going to grab me from behind. I turn my back to him, take a deep breath, and ready myself. "Now," he says once he wraps his arms around mine, pinning them at my side, "you want to grab your attacker's arms and pull them in."

He doesn't get to finish his explanation because my training kicks in, and I kind of zone out. Swinging my hips to the side, I shift my body, make a fist and land a solid punch to his groin area, which allows me to pivot around. Interlocking my hands behind the back of his neck, I proceed to bring my knee upwards and again strike him in the groin causing him to double over which gives me time to run. When I turn to flee, I don't get far because I face plant into Jake's chest.

"Little Bird," Jake grabs my attention.

I turn my head and look over my shoulder to find the instructor on one knee holding himself and catching his breath. *Shit.* "Grace," he coughs, "I think you should have warned me that you've had training before, that way I could have been better prepared," Rhett says standing.

A soft chuckle vibrates through Jake's chest as I bury my face. "You're fucking perfect," he rumbles.

15

JAKE

I'm on my way to the warehouse to meet up with Demetri, and some of the guys when my mind keeps playing the conversation I had with Grace this morning. Remi asked if Quinn could take her to school this morning so I called up my brother and asked him to come to my house first to pick her up instead of going straight to the bakery. Grace has gotten better about Remi riding on Quinn's bike. I, for one, was all for the change of plans this morning because it gave me the chance to make my woman scream without the worry of her daughter hearing us. And scream is what Grace did when I ate her pussy in the shower, making her come all over my face before I buried myself balls deep inside her from behind making her come a second time. Once we were done, she was quick to remind me that we once again did not use any protection.

"If I didn't know any better, I'd think you were purposely trying to knock me up," she jokes.

"I am," I tell her without a bit of humor in my voice. "And I think you want that too, don't ya, Little Bird?" Coming up behind her as she stands in the closet looking for something to wear, I place my hands on

her hips and let my breath fan the back of her neck when I speak again. "I think you like my cock bare inside that sweet pussy of yours. You like the idea of being round with my baby, don't ya?" I growl into her ear.

"Yes," she rasps, her body melting into mine. Her confession has made my cock hard once again, and I fuck her hard and fast against the wall giving us both what we want.

I wasn't lying when I said I wanted to knock her up. The first time we were together, it was not my intention, but since then, yeah, I would love a family with Grace. And if it doesn't happen, then I'm okay with that too. I have her; I have Remi, my club, and my brothers. I have nothin' to complain about.

It's been two weeks since the incident at the clubhouse with Liz, and Grace opening up to me more has made our relationship stronger. I feel I now have her complete trust, though the tension with her ex is still palpable. Not to mention the past two weeks of sittin' on our asses have been pure fuckin' torture.

The club has been waiting on Demetri's cargo and men to arrive before we make a move. O'Rourke has eyes in Chicago, and as of two days ago, all with the De Burcas' has been quiet. Ronan and his father have been in Boston for a week and arrived back in Chicago two nights ago. Our plan of attack is not an intricate one. O'Rourke knows Ronan's schedule like the back of his hand. Lucky for us, the motherfucker is a creature of habit. He has the same routine day in and day out; right down to the time of day he visits his whore each night.

Myself, Demetri, his men, along with Quinn, will fly out to Chicago by week's end. Grace knows what's comin' and is nervous and scared somethin' is going to happen to one of my men or me. I've tried talkin' to her and do everything I can to ease her mind, but I know my words fall on deaf ears.

I also made the call for Logan, Reid, and Gabriel to stay behind with the club. My boys did not like my decision, but in the end, they have small children and are just starting their families.

No way was I putting them in the kind of situation I was stepping into. After putting up a fight, all three relented and accepted what was. As their president, I will always put their best interests first.

A couple of years ago, I would not have thought twice about bringing them along, but now with them married and having families that depend on them I could not allow that. I don't know what to expect while in Chicago, all I know is one way or another I will end Ronan De Burca and my woman can finally be free.

Parking my bike next to Demetri's SUV, I cut the engine, climb off, and make my way inside. Taking my shades off, I place them on top of my ball cap and peer around the warehouse. My sights land on Logan first, who is standing next to Gabriel. I give both of them a chin lift before cutting my eyes to Demetri who is standing with Victor, his right-hand man along with four other men.

"Jake," Demetri greets, offering me his hand.

"Demetri," I return, "all this mine?" I ask, gesturing to the twelve crates stacked behind him.

"Yes. I have everything Quinn requested. I have to say I do like his taste."

"Fuckin' Quinn," I mutter under my breath, and that earns a few snickers from Logan and Gabriel. "Let's open these up and see what we got."

Using a drill, Victor opens the first crate. When I peer inside, I can't hold back my bark of laughter. "That little shit."

"What we got, Prez?" Logan asks, coming up beside me. "Hell, fuckin' yeah. This is what I'm talkin' about," he says, pulling an M79 40mm Grenade Launcher from the container, and I grab one as well.

"Is the plan still the same?" Demetri asks, bringing me out of my analysis of the M79.

"Yes, my original plan is still on course," I affirm, placing the weapon back in the crate.

"Prez, I want you to reconsider lettin' me in on this," Gabriel argues. "I don't like you going in without me havin' your back."

I give Gabriel my full attention. "I'm not changin' my mind on this one, son. I pulled Demetri and his men in on this for a reason. You and Logan are to stay in Polson with our family. I'm countin' on you all to keep everyone here safe. The club has never gone up against an organization as big as the De Burcas', and no way am I leavin' our women and children unprotected. Should things not go as planned, I will not be responsible for leaving those women and children without husbands and fathers. You got me, son?"

Running his tattooed hand through his hair, Gabriel sighs, "Yeah, Prez, I got ya."

LATER THAT NIGHT, I'm woken up by the sound of someone banging on my front door. Knifing up in bed, my body is on high alert. Peering at the clock on the table next to the bed, I see it's 1:00 am. *Who the fuck would be knocking on my door at this time?* Must be one of my brothers. By the persistent pounding, my guess is whatever it is that has them at my house is not good.

Getting out of bed, I snatch my jeans off the bedroom floor and tug them on. "Who is it, Jake?" Grace's sleep filled voice asks with concern. "Go back to sleep, baby. It's probably one of the guys."

Grace studies the clock and sits up a little straighter. "It's 1:00 am, Jake. Something must be wrong," she says, getting up and making her way into the closet and throwing on a pair of shorts and a t-shirt.

Knowing how stubborn my woman is, I don't argue with her as she follows me out of the bedroom and down the hall toward the front door. On the way, we pass Remi, who is standing at the end of the hallway by her room. "Mom, what's going on?"

At Remi's weary voice, Grace heads straight for her daughter. Giving Grace and Remi a reassuring smile, I continue my trek to the front of the house. Punching my code into the alarm panel, I swing the door open and bark, "You better have a good fuckin' reason for bangin' on my door at 1:00 am, brother," I tell a stone-faced Bennett. When I see Lisa standing behind him on my porch, I get a feeling of dread in my gut.

"What happened?"

"The garage is on fire, Jake."

"What the fuck? What the hell happened?" I ask over my shoulder while picking up my boots that were sitting by the front door and pull them on; then, I grab my cut and keys hangin' on the hook.

"I don't know what happened, Prez. Logan called me. He said he got a call from the alarm company, and that you weren't answering your phone. Then told me to get my ass over here. Logan, Gabriel, and all the other guys are headed there now."

I turn to Grace. "You stay here. I need to go deal with this shit," then turn to Bennett and Lisa, "Will you two stay here with Grace and Remi?"

"No!" Grace rushes out. "I'm going."

"No fuckin' way, babe. It's too dangerous. I want you here with Bennett." But as she goes about lacing up her tennis shoes, I know there will be no arguing.

"Fuck," I growl under my breath. "Bennett, will you and Lisa stay with Remi?"

Lisa answers, "Of course, we will."

Grace rushes back over to her daughter and whispers something in her ear, and Remi nods, hugging her mom.

Hopping in my truck, I peel out of the driveway and head toward the garage. We are a mile away from Kings Custom, and I can already see the smoke and flames. "Son of a bitch!" I curse and pound my hand on the steering wheel. At the same time, Grace gasps from the passenger seat and covers her mouth with her hand. When the garage comes into full view, we're met with two fire trucks and several police cars. Parking next to one of the squad cars, I take Grace's hand in mine and motion for her to slide out of the truck on my side. "Stay close to me, baby."

Rounding the hood of my truck, I'm met with Logan, Gabriel, Reid, and Quinn. My boys look tired as fuck, and the look in Logan's eyes is one of defeat but also suspicion. "Do any of you know what the hell happened here?"

"Fuck, Prez. No clue," Logan says. "By the time I got the call from the alarm company and got here, the whole fuckin' place was ablaze. Everything is gone, Jake. Fuck," he says, running his hand down his face and hangs his head.

Several hours have passed, and the only thing the guys and I can do is watch as Kings Custom burns to the ground. Fifty-five years of Delane history—of my life gone in a matter of hours.

"Are you Jake Delane?" a man in a fire suit asks me.

"Yeah, man, that's me," I reply, offering my hand.

"I'm Chief Sims. I wanted to come to introduce myself and catch you up on the situation," he tells me, shaking my hand.

"I want to start by saying I appreciate the hard work you and your men did to try and save my garage."

"You're welcome, Mr. Delane. We're just doing our job. I'm sorry we couldn't save the place."

"Any idea what caused the fire?" Reid cuts in.

He shakes his head. "It's hard to say without further investigation. Officer Carver said the alarm company was alerted to a possible break-in. With that being said, we can't rule out arson. I'll be heading the investigation and will get back with you and Polson PD."

At the mention of arson, my body tenses, and I see my brothers have the same reaction. "You sayin' someone purposely burned my garage down?"

"Yes, sir, that's what I suspect. I'll know more by the end of the day tomorrow. Unless you gentlemen have any more questions for me, I need to get back to work."

"No, Chief, no more questions. Thanks again."

With that, he goes back to help his men deal with the massive fuckin' mess at hand. A few seconds later, I realize Grace has gone quiet, and I also recognize the death grip she has on my hand. Looking at her, I see she has lost all color in her face.

"Baby, what's wrong?" I ask, pulling her into me. When she doesn't answer and continues to stare at me like she's not even seeing me, I give her shoulder a slight shake.

"Little Bird, talk to me."

Moments later, she comes back to me and chokes out, "It was him."

"What?" I ask but have a feeling I already know the answer.

"It's Ronan. He found me, and he's here. This is him letting me know." Grace sobs with tears running down her face.

"Baby, we can't know for sure this was him. The club has had eyes on him. Ronan is in Chicago." I try to reassure her, but Grace shakes her head, frantically back and forth. "No, Jake. It's him. You always tell people to trust their gut instinct. Well, I'm telling you my gut, and everything that is in me says he did this."

This time Grace's look is one of pleading. She needs me to believe her; I do. When I turn my attention back to my brothers, I see they overheard what Grace said, and they too believe her. Without wasting time, I begin barking orders. "Logan, Gabriel, and Reid, you three haul ass home. Pack up your woman and kids and get your asses back to the clubhouse, we're on lockdown. Quinn, you get on the phone and have Blake go to Sam and Leah's apartment, I want them at the clubhouse as well. Then have Austin find out if Emerson is at home or work, tell him to escort her to the clubhouse. This motherfucker has no problem going after anyone associated with the club or us, so that means I want your parents and sister on lockdown too. We're not taking any chances. I'm going to call Bennett and Lisa, have them bring Remi in while Grace and I ride out to my folk's place. On the way there, I'll call O'Rourke and find out what the hell is going on with De Burca. I expect to see all of you back at the compound within an hour."

With the last of my orders handed out, my boys give me a chorus of, "Yes sir." Before they walk off, we are interrupted by O'Rourke's car flying into the garage parking lot. He barely gets the vehicle in park before jumping out of the driver's side with his phone to his ear, and he's making a beeline for Grace.

"It's Glory. She's in the hospital."

16

GRACE

I have to grab hold of Jake's forearm the moment Finn says Glory's name. The look on his face telling me all I need to know that something is wrong. The knot in the pit of my stomach starts to grow heavier with each breath I take as I wait for Finn to get off the phone.

"That was her father," Finn says on an exhale as he puts his phone away. "She's in the hospital. Shit, Grace, she's been attacked, and it's pretty bad," his eyes darted from mine to Jake, then back to me again.

"It was Ronan, wasn't it?" I ask, already knowing the answer.

"We don't know anything..." he tries to say, but I cut him off.

"Bullshit. You and I both know who did this." I wave my hands toward the licking flames from Jake's garage. "That is their work, and it's too much of a coincidence that my best friend is in the hospital, too," I proclaim.

With all the chaos around us, I take a deep breath. I'm no good to anyone if I lose my shit. Remi is safe for now. There is nothing that can be done that the fire department isn't already doing at this moment. I make my mind up. I know it's a risk, but I have to go to Glory. She put herself in harm's way for me, and now it's my turn to be by her side. "Someone needs to take me to North Dakota," I demand.

"Dammit, Grace, if this is Ronan's handy work, he'll be waiting for you to make a move," Finn does his best to explain, but I'm not having any of it. I'm fed up.

Grabbing my shoulders, Jake coaxes me to turn and face him. "Babe, I can't risk letting you go after all this."

"I'm not asking for yours or Finn's permission, Jake. I'm going," I defend my decision and stand my ground. His expression softens with my determination.

"Alright, let me make a few arrangements, then we can get on the road." Kissing my forehead, he leaves me standing with Finn.

"You know how dangerous this trip will be, Grace. If he knows where you are, he won't let up," Finn says with a sigh.

"I know, but I can't keep going on this way. He's taken too much of my life already, and I won't allow him to keep me in fear and on the run any longer. I damn sure won't let him hurt the people I love, and if that means putting myself in harm's way, then that's what I'll do," I finish as I keep my eyes on Jake, who now has his phone to his ear.

As we stand to watch the fire diminish under the pelting of the water, I feel a calm wash over me. For some reason, at this moment, I think this is a pivotal turning point in my life. I've got my life back, and I'm prepared to fight for it. I won't let demons from my past take up space with their existence any longer.

Jake slides his phone into his back pocket and walks back our way. "I've got things sorted here for now. Demetri and a couple of his men are coming with us. They have a couple large sized SUV's we can ride in," he tells Finn and me.

"And Remi?" I ask.

"We can stop by the clubhouse on our way, Little Bird," Jake says as we load into his truck, and Finn climbs into his to follow us.

The ride out to the compound is filled with silence. Both of us lost in thought.

When we arrive, I can't get out of the truck fast enough to check on my daughter. Jake grabs my hand in his and leads me inside and passes a few members of the club milling around near the bar, talking and straight up the stairs. We stop in front of a bedroom door, and he lightly taps on it. A second later, Lisa opens the door, and lets us pass. "How are you guys holding up?" she asks with a weary, tired smile.

"We're doing alright, Lisa. I take it everyone hasn't made it here yet?" Jake runs his hand through his messy hair and questions her.

"No. I imagine they should start showing up within the hour. You know it takes time to load up a whole family in the middle of the night. They'll get here soon enough," she pats him on his forearm.

"Where's Bennett? I need to talk with him before we leave," he asks Lisa.

Remi finally emerges from the bathroom and makes a beeline toward the bed where I have just sat down. Throwing her arms around my neck, she embraces me, and I hug her close. I can't imagine how frightened she has been with all this commotion going on. When she finally pulls herself from me, the scared look on her face breaks my heart. "Peanut, I need to go check on Aunt Glory. I need to know you'll be okay while I'm gone," I push her hair from her eyes.

"What's happened? Mom, is Aunt Glory in trouble? Is she okay?" she anxiously asks and pulls her legs into a criss-cross position on the bed.

I won't lie to her. "She's in the hospital. I need to go to her. She isn't alone. Her mom and dad are by her side," I explain.

"I want to come with you," her hand reaches out and grabs mine.

Shaking my head, I tell her, "No. You will be staying here. I'll make sure you can call me anytime. I don't know how long we'll be gone."

Her face gets stone cold. Anger takes the place of her fear, and she turns her head to stare at the wall. "He did this, didn't he?"

I don't answer her. I don't need to. Jake returns with Lisa trailing behind him. "Our ride is here, babe. We need to get on the road soon," he softly speaks, letting me know time isn't necessarily on our side.

Sighing, I try to console my daughter, "You are my number one concern. The safest place for you right now is here with Jake's men. They will keep you safe," I rub her arm, so she'll look at me.

Turning her head, she lets her shoulders slump. "I can call you whenever I want," she clarifies.

"Anytime." I pull her in for one more hug and a kiss on her forehead before standing. Lisa gives me a look of knowing and understanding. Leaving is hard, but I know she will be taken care of. Our new family would lay down their own lives for one of their own, and we happen to be lucky enough to be a part of them. Looking over my shoulder, I glance at Remi one last time as Lisa tucks her into bed and strokes her hair for comfort.

On our way downstairs, we pass Gabriel. "You ready?" Jake asks him.

"Just got Alba and the kids settled. Let me grab a few things from the shed out back, and I'll meet you and Demetri outside," Gabriel informs Jake.

A look passes between them, then they nod at one another, and we continue to head downstairs. "Where are you going to put everyone?" I ask curiously.

"We have plenty of room. The members with families will occupy the upstairs and single men will put a cot where they can find the space. The main reason I bought this old warehouse was to make sure we always had space for any situation. It's not the Ritz, but as long as everyone pitches in, we can manage to make the experience bearable for everyone," he says in a tired breath as he rolls his head and rubs his neck. A couple of feet from the door, Logan walks in with Bella, Sofia, and a sleeping Breanna.

"Hey, Prez, you about to head out?" he asks, switching the car seat in his hand from one to the other.

"Yeah, brother. You've got command until I get back. Keep me posted on what you and the guys find whenever the authorities get done with their investigation of the fire. And don't let my mom and pop over do anything," he orders.

"Got it," he answers before following his family up the stairs. Pausing, he looks back, "Oh, I believe Quinn is on his way. Once he gets here, we will have everyone. I'll do a roll call soon and let you know if we are all accounted for."

Jake nods, and we walk out the door. One of Demetri's men opens the door to the SUV, and we climb inside where Demetri is seated already. "Your man, Gabriel, opted to drive the other vehicle in front of us, along with Mr. O'Rourke," he motions with a slight nod of his head out the front windshield to the SUV.

"Yeah, he's not much for being the passenger. You bring some extra protection in the form of artillery?" Jake asks.

"I did," Demetri slides a black leather duffle bag from the seat beside him and proceeds to unzip it. He hands a couple of handguns to Jake, one which is smaller in size than the other. "Babe," he takes the clip from the gun, checks to make sure it and the chamber is empty before handing it to me. "This is a Glock 43 9mm. I want you to get the feel of it in your hands because I want you to carry this with you."

Turning it over in my hand, I feel the weight of it. It's light, and I like the grip on it. The last gun I held was more cumbersome than this one and the grip much too large for my small hands. I remove the clip, check the chamber, then replace the clip and check the safety before holding my arm outright to check the sight. Finn showed me how to handle a weapon when he taught me self-defense. I was terrified to hold that kind of power in my hand at first. I've seen first hand with the pull of a trigger how fast someone can extinguish someone's life. Finn felt knowing how to handle and accurately shoot one could mean life or death if Ronan ever got his hands on me again, and he was right. I'm lost in my head with the weight of the metal in my hands when Jake speaks.

"Good, I can tell you know your way with a gun. I was hoping O'Rourke was smart enough to teach you a little something about them as well." Demetri hands him another object, but I can't tell what it is right away. "Pull your shirt up under your breast, babe. I'm going to wrap this around your waist." He takes what looks like slimming wear and wraps it around my midsection and secures it in place. "There's a pocket right here," he points, and I look down to my side, "This is a concealing garment. I want you to load the gun and keep it on you at all times. We're at war, babe. We can't trust anyone right now. No matter what, you protect yourself. Got it," Jake says in earnest.

Handing me the box of bullets, I steadily load the rounds into the clip, secure the weapon, then slide it into the concealed pocket under my shirt. The whole time I feel Jake and Demetri's stare.

"Fuck, if that's not the sexiest damn thing I have ever seen a woman do," Jake remarks.

Since we have the bench seat to ourselves, I tuck myself into Jake's side and try to relax. "You go on ahead and rest, Little Bird. I'll wake you before we get to where we are going." Jake pulls me in tighter.

Demetri swivels his seat back around to face forward, and the smooth sound of tires on the pavement ends up lulling me to sleep.

．．．

NOT SURE HOW long I was out, but I wake to Jake's rough hand running along my arm. "Babe, we'll be at the hospital in roughly five minutes."

Pressing my back against the seat, I stretch my arms above my head, trying to work out the stiffness in my lower back and groan. Inhaling deep, the smell of coffee fills the air. "Mmm, I smell coffee." Retrieving a to-go cup from a cup holder, Jake hands me the drink. "I need to check on Remi," I tell him and bring the cup to my lips and take a sip.

"I talked to Bella when Logan called to update me on roll call about two hours ago. Remi's fine, babe. Bella said she finally went to sleep and was still resting. I'm sure she'll ask to call as soon as she wakes up," he assures me.

Demetri's driver pulls the truck around to drop us off at the entrance of the small county hospital. "I need to make some calls and tend to some business. I hope that your friend is well, Grace," Demetri announces as Jake opens the door.

"Thank you, Demetri," I give him a weak smile. I hope she will be okay too.

Sliding across the seat, I let myself out the same door as Jake. Taking my hand, he guides me toward the hospital doors. Finn is waiting for us as we round the bumper of the vehicle.

Since Finn arrived before me and Jake, he informs us, "I talked to her parents from her hospital room. They know we are here," then pauses, "she's stable, but they beat her pretty bad. Her parents want to have her transferred to a different facility with private care until she heals."

I shake my head, "She won't go for it. She's too independent and headstrong for that," I add.

"That she is," Finn grins. "Let's get inside. I don't like standing out here in the open."

Finn already has the room number, so we load the elevator to the third floor and walk down the short hallway stopping in front of room 224.

"Come on, sweetheart, be reasonable," I hear the voice of Glory's mother say.

Knocking softly, I push the door open and walk in, followed by Jake, then Finn. The smile on my best friend's face when she sees me doesn't diminish the dark purple and deep red bruises on her pretty face. Her left eye is halfway swollen shut, and her right is bloodshot. I hold back my tears because they do none of us any good.

"I need a good makeup artist, don't I?" she remarks, trying to make light of the situation as her hand goes to her face.

Returning a smile, I cross the room first to greet her mother, who stands at her side. "Mrs. Keller," I hug her, "how are you?" I ask. I haven't seen the two of them in two years.

"Oh, sweetie, it is so good to see you," she tells me in her soft voice. "You are much too thin," she holds me at arm's length, inspecting my appearance.

"Mom, she looks good, let her be," Glory fusses.

"Oh, hush," she looks over her shoulder and tells her daughter, "I've missed my girls. I have a right to fuss over both of you." Focusing her attention back on me, she asks, "How's Peanut?"

Not having a granddaughter of her own, she took to my daughter as she was hers. It saddened all of us when Ronan stopped allowing them to see us. "She's good. Growing like a weed and sassy just like my momma," I chuckle.

"Get over here and give an old man a kiss on the cheek," Mr. Keller, Glory's dad, grumps from the other side of the hospital room where he is sitting in a chair. Doing as he asks, I walk past the end of the bed, stopping in front of him. Bending, I kiss his whiskered cheek. I don't think I've ever seen him without a beard. It's so bushy Remi used to believe he was Santa Claus.

"Keeping yourself busy, Mr. Keller?" I stand and ask.

Letting out a grunt, he grumps, "As much as I can get away with without the enforcer over there cracking the whip on my old ass," he smirks, trying to get a rise from his wife. "You going to introduce us," he gestures behind me toward Jake.

"Mr. and Mrs. Keller, this is Jake Delane," I introduce them.

"Nice to meet both of you," he greets the two of them. Walking beside me, he gives Mr. Keller a firm handshake.

"And why are you here?" he asks him with his hand still clasped around his.

"I'm Grace's, man." Jake states.

Sizing Jake up, Mr. Keller gives Jake a look over. "Military?" He raises a bushy eyebrow.

"Yes, sir," Jake answers.

Satisfied, for now, Glory's dad nods his head and releases Jake's hand. "June dear, let's go get something to eat and let these youngsters chat."

After the two of them kiss their daughter on the cheek, they leave the room, closing the door behind them. Sitting down on the side of the bed, I grab Glory's hand. "Talk to me. Tell me who did this."

Glory's face turns ashen. I hate to have her relive the moment. I'm sure she's had to recount the moment more than once already, but we need to know.

"I stepped outside with Bo," she looks at Jake because he's the only one in the room who doesn't know who Bo is. "Bo is my basset hound," she smiles. "As soon as I turned my back, I felt a sharp blow to the back of my head, and then I was shoved inside. There were two of them," she looks to Finn, "They weren't very tall. I would say just under six foot each. One had black hair and was a bit lanky, and the other was bald, but I remember seeing a tattoo on the side of his neck." She pauses while she tries to recall what the tattoo looked like. "I think it was a dagger. I'm not one hundred percent sure," she closes her eyes and squeezes my hand but continues. "What felt like forever probably only lasted minutes. The only time one of them spoke was once I had come to after one of the last blows to my face." Opening her good eye, she locks eyes with me. "He said he's coming to take back what belongs to him."

My stomach sinks. I knew it. I knew it was Ronan. He sent his goons to relay a message that he knows where we are. "Glory, I am so sorry. This is all my fault," I confess and hang my head.

"Like hell, it is. They beat me. Not you. And before you try to say anything else, you know I'll disagree with, I'll say this too. I chose to help my best friend. No one made me do anything," she chastises.

Jake strides across the room to the window and peers out. Glory follows him with her eyes. "Honey, that man is fine." The entire hospital floor could have heard her attempt to whisper. Being amused, Jake chuckles to himself.

Clearing his throat Finn comes to stand on the opposite side of Glory. "You plan on taking your parents' advice and maybe skipping town or the country for a while?" he asks her.

"No," Glory crosses her arms, which causes her to wince from the pain. Catching me looking concerned, she says, "I have a few bruised ribs and a slight concussion, but other than that, I'm fine. And to answer your question Finn, no, I'm not. I'm not letting that piece of shit run me off. I'm stayin'."

I told them she was headstrong. As long as I've known her, she has always been persistent and gotten what she wanted. Her money never had anything to do with it. When she was determined to do something or have something, she would go after it until she got it.

"You're coming home with me," I declare. "If you don't want to leave town, then you need to have a safe place to stay. The only place I can think of is with me."

She shifts her attention to Jake, who continues to watch out the window. "So, Delane, you plan on protecting us from the De Burcas'? You'll have to end his life, or he'll never stop."

Stepping to my side, Jake possessively places his hand on my hip and peers down at me when he answers her. "War is nothing new to me, sweetheart. The motherfucker sealed his fate a long time ago. The De Burcas' don't know whose backyard they just stepped into. I'll gladly give my last breath to keep Grace and Remi —my family safe."

17

JAKE

On the long ass drive back to Polson, I can't help but reflect on the conversation I had with Glory's father. We were getting ready to leave the hospital, and I was on my way downstairs to pull the SUV around to the front entrance when Mr. Keller offered to ride the elevator down with me. Once inside and the doors closed, he turned toward me and asked me a question. A question I respectfully answered. This is a man who, even though he's not Grace's father, he, in a way, stepped in and took on the role after she lost hers. I knew without a doubt; this man loved Grace as if she was his real daughter.

"What do you love about Grace?" he asked in a no-bullshit tone.

Without skipping a beat, I looked him straight in the eyes, "I love everything about her. I love her strength, her courage, her unwavering spirit to live. I love the way she reasons with logic but is not afraid to challenge it. I love the way she puts the people she loves first. But most of all, I love all the broken pieces of her soul. They fit together with the broken pieces of mine. Apart we were like jagged little pieces not fitting in with any puzzle. No matter how hard you try to force them to fit, they don't go. I knew the moment I walked into Grace's bakery she was my piece. I knew the moment she looked at me with those wounded, fiery blue eyes she was my person. The one who completes the missing pieces of my soul. I also knew her pieces were a little broken. So, I spent two years gluing them back together. And it was worth every single second."

By the time I was finished with my little speech, I knew I had given him the answer he was looking for and more. I had meant every word. If he was shocked that a man like me, a hardened biker, President of The Kings of Retribution motorcycle club, so easily laid his feelings out there, then he didn't let on. I'm not sure what kind of answer he was expecting from someone like me. Hell, maybe he thought I would say something like I love how beautiful she is or some superficial muck like that. If a man gives that kind of shit as his answer, then he has no idea what love is. Love is looking beyond the exterior. None of us are perfect. We all have a fuck ton of flaws. It is our flaws that make us unique. When you find yourself obsessed with the individual parts of the person you are with, then that is how you know it's love. When you witness a person go through some of the worst shit in their lives and they are at their lowest, but to you, they have never been more beautiful, that is love. Take Grace's scars, for example. To her, they are ugly, but to me, they are symbols of strength. Her scars show she survived what was trying to break her. My Grace is unbreakable, and to me, that is the sexiest thing about her.

I'm pulled from my thoughts when I hear whispers coming from the back seat of Demetri's SUV we are riding in. Cutting my eyes over my shoulder, I see Grace fussing over Glory and Glory, rolling her eyes. I know Grace is feeling guilty for what happened to her friend. Ronan sure did a number on her too, but it's not Grace's fault. The fact that her friend took a beating and still didn't give up any information on Grace has told me all I need to know about Glory and the kind of friend she is. To hear them talk and see them together, I know they are more like sisters. I have no doubt Glory would have given her life to protect Grace. The fact Ronan was able to find Grace has Glory struggling with her guilt. And that too is weighing heavy on my Little Bird's heart.

I direct my attention away from my woman when my phone alerts me to an incoming text. Pulling it from my cut, I see it's Logan updating me on how things are back at the clubhouse. He's been keeping me informed every few hours. Bella and the rest of the women have been doing an excellent job at keeping Remi busy and her mind off her mom. The kid is smart; she knows her father is a bad man and is behind what happened to my garage. She's also worried something will happen to her mom. It will be a cold day in hell before I let anything happen to Grace or my family.

It's been a few years since the club has been on lockdown and even longer since we've had to bring in the entire family. Luckily the clubhouse is huge and able to house everyone comfortably without feeling like we are all on top of each other. Logan said none of the families put up a fight when told to get their asses there for which I am not surprised. My parents, along with Quinn's mom and dad, know we would not ask such a thing unless it was a matter of life and death.

There is one son of a bitch who thought he could come into my town and threaten what's mine. I feel my body tense and my blood heat at the thought of getting to wrap my hands around the bastard's throat and slowly watching the life drain from his eyes. And I will do so with pleasure.

"All good, back home?" Demetri asks from the front seat.

"Yeah, brother. Logan says things have been quiet since we left."

Giving me a curt nod, Demetri then glances over my shoulder and into the back at Glory. Something he has been doing non-stop since we have been on the road. The funny thing is, he's not even subtle. He's blatant about it, and we all watch Glory squirm under his gaze. If I'm not mistaken, I believe he has taken an interest in Grace's friend. The first clue was back at the hospital after Glory's parents declined my offer to stay with us in Polson, Demetri immediately stepped in once he saw the worry on Glory's face and insisted that one of his men watch over her parents until the situation with Ronan has been handled. Not wanting to upset his daughter any further, Mr. Keller accepted Demetri's offer. We can all rest a bit easier knowing her parents are protected.

There is also another look in my friend's eyes when he's watching Glory. It's a look I know all too well. Demetri lost the love of his life a long time ago. I'm willing to bet what he is feeling for Glory is something he's not felt since Rose, and he doesn't quite know what to do with those feelings. Like me, he's probably assumed he'd never feel for another woman the way he felt for the woman he once loved and lost.

It's nearly nightfall when we arrive back at the clubhouse. When we pull up to the gate, Blake and Austin greet us, both armed and on high alert, just as I would expect.

"Wow," Glory breathes when she takes in her new surroundings. "You all sure don't play around, do ya?" she remarks when she notices our security. Not only do we have Blake and Austin at the front gate, but we also have Reid and our new prospect Grey on the roof armed and ready for anything and welcoming us in the parking lot is Logan, Bennett, and Nikolai.

"Good to see ya make it back okay, Prez," Logan says as I slide out of the SUV. Clapping him on the back, "Thanks for holding things down here while I was gone, son."

"What the hell do y'all put in the water 'round here?" Glory jests as Grace helps her out of the truck behind me.

"Girl, they sure do know how to grow them in Montana. At least I'll have some decent eye candy while we're in lock-up," she jokes while taking in all my brothers.

"Glory!" Grace whisper hisses. "You can't say stuff like that. Some of these men are married."

"Not all of them, though, right?"

"Oh lord, let's just get you inside and settled," Grace huffs exasperated at her friend and Glory giggles.

Walking into the clubhouse, Remi launches herself at full speed into her mom's waiting arms. "I was so scared, Mom."

"Oh Peanut, there's nothing to be scared of. I was safe the whole time. Jake wouldn't let anything happen to me."

Hearing Grace's words of confidence to her daughter that I would protect her fills me with pride. Leaning in, I whisper into her ear, "Why don't you, Remi, and Glory go upstairs and catch up. I'm going to make my rounds with the family. Once you all have talked and settled in, you can come back down and meet everyone."

"Thank you, Jake."

"You're welcome, babe. Now go on. I'll have the prospect bring Glory's bags up in a minute." I say, giving her a soft kiss on her lips, and she melts into my touch.

Several minutes later, I begin making my way around the clubhouse to check up on the family. My first stop was my parents, who I found in the kitchen along with Raine and Ember who were busy setting up for dinner. Ma was showing the girls how to make her homemade peach cobbler while my dad sat at the table drinking coffee. Leaving the kitchen, I run into Quinn. "Hey son, I was looking for your folks. I wanted to say hi and see how they are doing."

"Hey, Prez. They're out back. I was just headed that way myself." Following him down the hall and out the back door, I see Bella, Alba, Mila, Emerson, and Leah all hanging with kids and watching them play. With them is Quinn's mom. Victoria is a beautiful African American woman with shoulder-length hair and stunning honey color eyes. She's also a tiny little thing standing no taller than 5 feet 2 inches. But don't let her size fool ya. That woman is a firecracker. She has to be with a son like Quinn. On the other side of the yard sitting around the fire pit, is his dad Quinten. He has light brown salt and pepper hair and stands a couple of inches shorter than me. I decide to make my way over to the ladies first. When I approach, Victoria gives me a big warm smile.

"Vicky, get your ass over here and give me a hug," I say, returning her smile.

"It's been awhile JD, how have you been?" I've known Quinn's parents as long as I've known him. JD is what Victoria has been calling me for years. "My son tells me you went and fell in love. Where is the lucky lady?" she asks, hugging me.

"She'll be down in a bit. In the meantime, I wanted to see how you were holding up. You or Quinten need anything you let me know, sweetheart."

"We're fine, JD. You focus on taking care of business. Quinn didn't tell us too much of what was going on. But Quinten and I trust you, and when you said to get here and get here fast, that's what we did."

"I appreciate that, Vicky. And I promise the boys and I are going to handle the situation soon."

"You over here, flirting with my girl?" I hear a voice question, and when I turn, I see Quinten walking up behind me.

"I'm tryin' too, but she's not buyin'." I hedge, holding out my hand for him to shake.

"It's good to see you, Jake," Quinten says, shaking my offered hand.

"You too, man. I was telling Vicky I appreciate you all coming to stay here for a few days."

"No problem. You know we'd do anything for the club."

After spending several minutes talking with Quinn's parents, I walk around the yard and have a few words with all my brothers, then I stop and get my grandpa love from the kids. Across the yard, I spot Sam sittin' in a chair with a beer in his hand and his eyes on Sofia, who is down on the ground playing with the kids.

"Hey, kid," I say, taking the seat next to him.

"How's it going, Mr. Delane?"

"You want to tell me what that's all about?" I ask tilting my head toward Sofia.

At my question, the boy actually blushes and takes a pull of his beer. "And I don't care what Alba and Leah say; I don't believe for one second you're gay, not that any of us would care. But no way do I believe that shit with the way you look at that girl." No sooner do the words leave his mouth when Sam chokes on his drink and beer sprays out of his mouth.

"Gay! My friends think I'm gay? What the hell!"

Chuckling, I hold my hands up in mock surrender. "Hey, don't shoot the messenger. Besides, the guys and me never thought for a second, you were gay. Especially not with all the interest you've been showing Sofia." When Sam goes to open his mouth, I hold up my hand cutting him off. "Look kid, I'm not here to bust your balls, but I will say if you hurt that girl, I will personally cut your dick off and feed it to ya."

"I would never hurt Sofia, Mr. Delane."

"Good. Keep it that way, kid, because I like ya and would hate to have to hurt ya."

On the way back inside, I notice Emerson propped up against the side of the clubhouse nursing a beer, and she has her eyes trained on Quinn and his parents.

"How ya holdin' up, sweetheart?" I ask, saddling up beside her and taking a pull of my beer.

"I'm doing okay, Jake. How's Grace's friend? You know if you need me to look at her or anything, don't hesitate to ask."

"Thanks, darlin'. I think she's okay for now, though. Maybe see how she's feeling tomorrow."

After giving me a nod, we're both quiet for a moment before I speak up again. "You're wondering about his parents, aren't ya?"

"Am I that obvious?"

Chuckling, I shake my head. "Darlin', you and Quinn have been dancin' around each other for too long now. One thing you should know by now is Quinn is an open book. You only need to turn the pages. I promise you won't be disappointed with what you find. I'm almost certain you want him just as much as he does you, and you're holdin' back. And I get it, I do. Lovin' one of us men means lovin' the club. For most, that is a scary thought. But one thing I know for sure is that you won't find a better man than Quinn, and you won't find a more loyal family than The Kings." After kissing the top of her head, I leave her to chew on my words.

18

GRACE

You would think with all these members under one roof, there would be complete chaos, but there isn't any of that. I also would have thought Glory would be overwhelmed with so many people, but that's not the case either. If anything, she seems to be more at ease than she was before we got here last night. And although Remi can't leave to attend school until all this is over, I hope it's sooner than later, she has been enjoying herself. Remi has quickly made friends with Quinn's baby sister Katalina, but she prefers to be called Kat. We met her parents, Quinn's mom and dad yesterday. They are a beautiful and sweet couple.

Softly knocking on the bedroom door to the room Glory is occupying, I wait for her to answer before turning the handle and opening the door. Poking my head inside, I find her sitting on the side of the twin size bed. "Hey, how are you feeling this morning?"

"Aside from the tight muscles in my back and side, I feel like I need a two-hour soak in a hot bath." Her eyes lock with mine, "Seriously, I feel pretty good," Glory replies as she reaches for the glass of water and the plastic pill bottle sitting on her nightstand.

Having not yet stepped into the room, I ask, "Would it be okay if a doctor friend came in and gave a look at you this morning."

Glory pops the pill in her mouth and tips the glass up. "I don't mind. Does this doctor look like the rest of those delicious looking bikers I met last night?"

Swinging the door open, I step inside, and Emerson walks in behind me then closes the door. "Afraid not," Emerson laughs.

"Glory, this is Emerson," I introduce the two. Emerson takes a seat on the edge of the bed next to Glory. "Dr. Evans, Grace has told me about you and the rest of the girls she's been lucky enough to become friends with. I'm happy to meet one of you finally," Glory gives her a sincere smile.

"You'll get to meet the rest of them soon," Emerson tells her. "You mind if I take a look at your side?" she asks Glory. Lifting the hem of her shirt, Glory exposes her ribs, and I cringe. The bruises on her side vary in color from dark purples to reds and cover all her exposed skin on her side.

Lightly touching the traumatized area, Emerson examines her. Moving on, she cleans the stitches on the back of Glory's head. "No signs of infection, but still a little swelling. That warm bath you spoke of a few minutes ago is a great idea. It will help relax the tense muscle spasms you're having in your back."

Knocking at the door draws our attention. Cracking the door slightly open, Remi pokes her head in. "Momma, are we allowed to go outside?" she asks.

I haven't heard Jake say otherwise, but to be safe, I think I need to discuss it with him first. The compound is secluded, but that doesn't mean the area isn't prone to being vulnerable. Yesterday everyone was outside, and I was less worried. This morning with everyone still indoors, I'd prefer her not to be out there. "Peanut, I don't think it's a good idea right now, but I'll see what Jake has to say about you guys going outside for some fresh air."

A deep sigh leaves her lips. "Fine, I guess I'm going to go find Kat and hang out with her and watch some Netflix."

Crossing the room, I open the door a bit and pull her in for a hug. "I know this whole situation sucks." Throwing her head back, Remi looks at me. I push the mass of curls from her face.

"Are you and Aunt Glory coming down to eat breakfast? I helped make the French toast casserole," she smiles.

"Of course, I'm going to run her a bath; then I'll head to the kitchen and help the rest of the women. Lord knows we have several mouths to feed and tons of food to cook," I tell her. Peeking around my shoulder, Remi says, "See you downstairs, Aunt Glory," then rushes off to find Kat.

"That kid is my favorite person," Glory remarks.

"You're biased," I tell her and head toward the bathroom.

"Damn right, I am," Glory smiles.

"Alright, ladies. I'm going to leave you to it." Standing, Emerson grabs her medical bag. "I'll see you both later. My shift starts in about two hours, and I have a feeling I'm going to have to sneak out of here to get there." She walks out the door and closes it behind her. She's right. Emerson is going to have a fight on her hands getting the men—one man, in particular, to let her leave with everything that's going on. I hate that my baggage has affected them and permanently put everyone's life on hold for the moment. I've watched my friends overcome many obstacles over the years. The last thing I wanted to do was add to it.

"What's with the melancholy look on your face," Glory starts to move toward the bathroom.

"We are stuffed in this building like sardines because of my past, Glory. That doesn't bother you at all?"

Pulling the shower curtain back, I turn the hot and cold water on and start filling the small tub.

"Why would it bother me?" She shrugs. "Look, life sucks sometimes. Right now, Ronan and his merry men happen to be the ones leaching on it for all it's worth right now. So, we do what we need to do and use the help you've been given to our advantage. You were lucky enough to get away from that piece of shit and his family. Sure, two years of hiding has been tough, but you are alive. Remi is alive."

Plopping down on the toilet seat, I take in my best friend's words. Peeling off her clothes, she steps into the water and lowers herself.

"Oh my god," she moans as the warmth of the water relaxes her. "You have several large badass bikers on your side. I have a feeling the De Burca family has met their match, and I, for one, can't wait to see all of them go straight to hell." Closing her eyes, Glory sinks a little further into the water.

"Hell would be too good for the likes of Ronan De Burca," I murmur. Standing, I announce, "I'm gonna head downstairs and get busy cooking. Come find me when you're done," I tell her before leaving her to enjoy her bath in peace.

When I make my way downstairs, I find the common area taken over by many of the member's kids of various ages playing, watching TV, or playing video games. Turning to my left, I walk through the kitchen door and find Bella, Alba, and Raine milling around, trying to get brunch ready.

"Hey, Grace, thank god you're awake. We could use an extra pair of hands in here," Bella announces as she pulls waffles from the iron then ladles more batter onto the hot surface before closing it tight.

"Put me to work." Taking the hair tie from my wrist, I pull my mess of hair away from my face and secure it in a low ponytail. Glancing around the kitchen, I notice someone missing. "Where, Lisa?"

"Oh, Bennett took her to the grocery store. We've run out of bread and a few other items. They should be back before too long." Alba tells me as she hands her and Bella's daughter the toys they keep throwing over the edge of the playpen they have set up on the other side of the kitchen.

Roughly an hour later, we have finished cooking. The kitchen door creaks open, and Quinn pops his head in. "We got the tables set up. You ladies need a hand?"

"Thanks, Quinn," says Bella, who has two casserole dishes in her hands. Walking up to her, Quinn takes them from her and carries them out to the common room. Soon after, Blake walks in to help us as well. With a little help, we get everything laid out across three tables, including the paper plates and plasticware. As the mommas go about plating some food for the smaller kids first, Jake walks up behind me and wraps his arms around my middle and leans down placing a light kiss on my neck. I let my eyes close for a moment enjoying the connection. Of all the ways he touches me, this—a light caress of his lips on my neck, is my favorite.

"You smell so good, Little Bird," Jake murmurs.

Hearing a shuffle behind me, I peer around Jake's arm to see Glory making her way down the stairs. "Okay, people. I smell bacon," she announces.

"I put some aside for you in the microwave just in case you didn't make it down in time," I laugh.

"You are the best," she pauses, grabs both sides of my face and plants a kiss on my lips. The gesture is nothing unusual to me. She's done this as long as we've known each other. She can be dramatic about it, but that's how we are. She's my ride or die bestie. However, the lip action catches the attention of a couple of other people, one being Quinn, who makes his feelings known on the public display of affection.

"Do it again," he begs, holding a plate full of waffles and scrambled eggs as he stares in our direction. Adding fuel to his fire, true to Glory's nature, she blows him a kiss and smiles.

"Don't encourage him," Jake chuckles. "Besides, I don't want Demetri to kill one of my men," he lifts his chin, gesturing across the room. Glory and I follow his line of sight. Completely zoned in on my best friend with a stare so intense, even I can feel the heat, is Demetri. When I lift my eyes to Glory, her death stare in his direction is in full force. He has no idea what he wants to go after. Glory is one of a kind—a force of nature. Demetri better be prepared for a chase because Glory will be a hard one to catch.

"That man wants to devour you," I whisper in her direction.

"Yeah, well, too bad for him. I'm not interested. I'll be in the kitchen," Glory says, breaking their connection and walking away.

"Did you believe a word she said?" Jake questions me as we continue to watch everyone eat.

"Not a word," I state.

"Come on," he grabs my hand, "Let's get some food before they eat it all." About the time we grab a couple of plates, the front door burst open, causing it to slam into the wall creating a loud thud. In stumbles, a bloodied Bennett assisted by Austin.

"Prez, he's been shot," Austin yells.

Struggling to stand, Bennett rages, "Jake, they got Lisa. Those motherfuckers took my woman."

19

JAKE

"What the fuck!" I curse, rushing over to my lifelong friend. "Emerson, I need you over here now!" I shout, but it wasn't necessary because she is by my side and in front of Bennett in seconds. "What the fuck happened, brother?" I ask a bloodied and battered Bennett as I reach out to him. Unable to move any further, he lays on his back, sprawled out on the clubhouse floor. It's then I hear the gurgled sounds of his voice as he tries to speak.

"Motherfucker got my old lady, Jake. They have my wife. They ambushed us about two miles down the road. Rammed into us from behind and we ended up in a ditch. The next thing I know is the window being smashed in, and some motherfucker knocks my woman out and pulls her out the passenger window. I got one shot off, hitting the guy before a couple of shots were fired into my window. I'm pretty sure the guy I hit is still there. Fuckers left him behind." He spits out passed the blood in his mouth.

Jerking my head up, I look at Logan and Gabriel. "You two go see what's left behind. If that son of a bitch Bennett popped is still alive, bring his ass in. You know what to do."

Looking at the rest of the room, I see the children and family members have cleared out. Thank fuck, because I don't want anyone, especially children, to have to witness this shit. I turn my attention back to Emerson, who has ripped open Bennett's button-down shirt exposing a bubbly bloody hole in his left rib cage.

"Goddammit! He's been shot," she shouts. "He has a collapsed lung. He's going to need to go to the hospital now. I can't fix this here."

"In my room," Bennett grinds out through his pain. "The duffel bag in my closet."

"Already on it!" Reid rushes into the room, dropping a large bag by Emerson's side.

"He needs surgery to remove the bullet. I can't do this here, Jake," she says with fear and slight uncertainty in her voice.

"No time doc. You gotta do it, yeah? I need ya to save my brother." I watch as Emerson closes her eyes briefly, and when she opens them a second later, they are filled with fire and determination. Without missing a beat, she reaches over and unzips the bag Reid brought; she goes to work, pulling out a package and ripping it open. "This is going to hurt like a bitch without any pain medicine," she warns and then proceeds to take a bottle of rubbing alcohol and splashes it across Bennett's ribs and chest. She then takes a pair of forceps and inserts them into the hole in his chest. A roar and a string of curses come from my brother's mouth the same time Emerson pulls the forceps from his body along with the bullet. Next, she takes a scalpel and cuts an incision between two of his ribs before she uses a pair of small scissors and slides them through the cut she just made. The clubhouse is eerily quiet aside from Bennett's labored breathing as Emerson rips open another package, this one containing a tube. She then takes the scissors out of Bennett's ribs and replaces it with the tube. Once it's in place a gush of blood passes through it and onto the clubhouse floor, and instantly Bennett's breathing gets better.

Now that the most urgent care is over with, Emerson moves on to the other visible injury. My brother's right ear has been nearly severed from the side of his head.

"Bullet," Emerson mutters to me as she uses some gauze and tape to hold it in place. "I can sew it back on just as soon as we get him off the floor and moved somewhere more comfortable. I also need to get him something for the pain before going any further."

"I don't want to get more comfortable. I want you to finish patchin' me up, so I can go find my wife," Bennett bites out as he begins to scramble on the floor like he is trying to get up.

"Lay your ass back down, brother. You're not going anywhere with a tube stickin' out of your damn chest. We're going to find Lisa. I promise you that."

Bennett tries to sit up in protest once again. And I can't blame him. Lisa is his world, and right now, he feels as though his world has come crashing down. But no way is he in any condition to fight. "Bennett, you know I love ya, and you're my brother, but right now, I'm talkin' to ya as your President. You stay put and let Emerson fix you up." I don't miss the flash of anger on his face as he takes in my words. He's not happy with my call, but he'll respect and abide by it.

"Prospect!" I bark.

"Prez?" Grey says, walking up to me.

"I want you to help Blake and Emerson get Bennett moved to his room, so she can finish fixing him up."

"You got it, Prez."

Once they make their way out of the room, I turn to Reid. "See what you can find out on Lisa's cell. Maybe we'll get lucky, and she still has it on her. Not likely, but it's worth a shot." Nodding his head, he turns on his heel on a mission. Standing in the middle of the empty clubhouse room, I look down at the floor to where my best friend's blood is, and then I tip my head back and suck in a deep breath. Lisa is the matriarch of this club. She is essential and irreplaceable. I love the woman like a sister, and I vow to bring her home safely. Right after I kill any man, who would dare think they can fuck with my family.

"Jake, my friend. Can my men or I be of some service?" Demetri asks, coming up behind me. Turning to face him, I peer over his shoulder to see Victor and another one of his men standing at the entrance of the room.

"I need eyes on the town. Can you have your men drive around, see what they can find? You all have been in Polson long enough to know a local from a newcomer. Leave no stone unturned. If your men can handle that, I'd like for you to join me in church when Logan and Gabriel return."

"I can do that," he says, inclining his head and making his way back across the room to his men to dish out instructions. At this point, we don't have shit to go on. Having eyes on the town looking for anything suspicious is better than not doing anything at all. I hope to God Reid comes back with a lead. And as much as I want the fucker that Bennett shot to be burnin' in hell right about now, I'm hoping he's still got some life in him, just enough for us to get some intel out of him. Once I get what I need from him, I'll gladly assist him on meetin' his maker. Out of the corner of my eye, I catch Raine walking into the room with a bucket of water and a mop. She strolls right up to the bloody fuckin' mess on the floor and begins cleaning. Striding up to her, I gently palm her face and kiss the top of her head. Raine and Ember have been a godsend to the club. The old ladies have taken a shinin' to the girls too. Probably because they both are respectful. They stay away from the taken men, and they never have to be told what to do. Like now, for example. In the past, the club girls we had made it hard to respect them. We don't treat any woman who walks through these doors like they don't matter. Whether you're an old lady or a club girl, you are respected. The problem with Cassie and Liz was they fucked up too many times to count and lost that respect. "Thanks, sweetheart. Don't know what this club would do without ya."

"I could say the same thing about you all," she replies with a weak smile. "You guys have been amazing to Ember and me. And the women don't look down their noses at us. I can't speak for Ember, but I don't know where I'd be right now without the club."

I give her shoulders a light squeeze. "Where is Ember?"

"She's helping the women with the kids. They were pretty shaken up by what went down a little bit ago, and she knew they would need some help keeping them distracted. Especially Grace. I think you should go check on her," she adds.

"Yeah, I think that's a good idea. Do me a favor. When Logan and Gabriel get back, will you tell them I said meet me in church?"

"Sure, Jake. I'll tell them."

Making my way to the back of the clubhouse, I walk into the entertainment room we had built last year for all the kids. The children look to me none the wiser as to what's going on, aside from Remi. I can tell by the terrified look on her face she knows this all has to do with her father. And the devastated look of guilt on my Little Bird's face says she knows too. Walking over to the couch where she and Remi are huddled together, I drop down to my knees in front of Grace, and she throws her body into mine and sobs into my neck.

"I'm so sorry, Jake. This is all my fault. If it weren't for me, none of this would be happening to you all. Bennett was nearly killed, and Lisa is gone."

Sensing we need a minute, Bella comes up behind me. "Hey, Remi, we're headed to the kitchen to fix the kids some ice cream. Why don't you come with us?"

When Remi cuts her weary eyes over to me, I give her some encouragement. "It's okay, darlin'. I got your momma. Go on with Bella and the other women."

Once the room has cleared, I tip Grace's chin back to where she is looking straight at me. "What have I said about hearin' you say shit like that? Now you hear me, and you hear me good, babe. Nobody—not one person here blames you for a damn thing. You and Remi mean everything to me, and you mean somethin' to the club. You two are family. And we will fight your son of a bitch ex to the depths of hell to keep you safe."

"I'm safe right now, Jake. But what about Lisa? Ronan is a cruel man. I can't stand the thought of what he might be doing to her right now."

"Lisa is a strong woman, Grace. She'll survive and get through this. I don't want you thinkin' any different. We're going to find her and bring her home. I promise ya that."

"All Ronan wants is me," she says, hanging her head, "so I should..." I effectively cut her off.

"Not fuckin' happenin', babe. You will not be offerin' yourself up to that man. So, you best get that idea out of your gorgeous head right now and do not let me hear you talk like that again."

"Excuse me, Jake," Raine interrupts by knocking on the door. "Logan and Gabriel are back, and so is Reid. They asked me if I'd find you and let you know. They said they'd be in church."

"Thanks, darlin'," I express, and she leaves.

I shift my attention back to Grace. "The boys and I got church. We're going to settle this shit once and for all and bring Lisa home." Cupping her face in my hands, I claim her lips with mine. "I love you, Little Bird."

"I love you too, Jake."

SLAMMING the gavel down on the table, I don't hesitate to get down to business. "What'd you and Gabriel find?" I turn my head to look at Logan.

"Got the motherfucker Bennett popped. He's still breathin' too.

Gabriel carted his ass down to the basement. Grey is watching over him now."

"Is he talkin'?" I ask.

"Not yet," Gabriel gruffs, stretches his arms, and cracks his knuckles. "But he will be."

Fuck yeah, he will. He'll be singing like a canary by the time I get done with him.

"Reid, what ya got for me?"

"Sorry, Prez. I didn't get any hits off Lisa's cell."

Logan speaks. "Her purse and cell were in the truck."

"Alright, men. Here is what's going down. Demetri has his men canvassing the town. Reid, I want you to keep doing what you do best. Tap into the fuckin' traffic cams if you have to. Look for anything out of the norm. These motherfuckers may be slick, but I'd bet they're not smart enough to drive around in inconspicuous vehicles. Their pussy asses are probably in SUVs. You know Polson locals don't have that high-class shit. No offense, brother," I say, directing my statement at Demetri. He and his men are probably the only ones in Polson who stick out like a sore thumb. The smirk on my friend's face tells me he's not offended.

"Quinn, I want you and Austin to go to the warehouse and load up. I want you back here by the time I get done with the asshole in the basement. It's time for war brothers," I proclaim, slamming the gavel.

With Logan and Gabriel on my heels, I walk into the basement of the clubhouse and am met with Grey, who is sitting in a chair in front of our new industrial freezer. Something we had installed a year ago.

"Open it up," I order.

When Gabriel steps in front of me, he opens the freezer door, and in front of us is the man who damn near killed my best friend. He's strung up by his wrists in nothing but his boxers. A gunshot wound is evident on his shoulder, and his skin has already begun to turn a nice shade of blue. Reaching into my pocket, I pull out my brass knuckles, because I'm old school like that. Slipping them on over my right hand, I stride toward my prey as I flex my fist a few times. Rearing back, I swing and land my first blow to his left cheek, and I get a sick feeling of satisfaction when I feel bones crunching, and his skin splits open, causing his blood to spray all over my fist.

"Where is she?" I growl a mere inch from his face. My question only earns me a mouth full of blood spit at my feet, and that earns him a blow to his kidney, and he roars out in pain. The motherfucker is sure to be pissin' blood the next time he takes a leak. Too bad for him, he won't be living long enough to find out. I land blow after blow, and my arm is feeling the burn. The guy's face is unrecognizable.

"You think you low life bikers are a match for the De Burcas'?" the man sneers a garbled response past his busted lips and broken teeth. "My loyalty lies and dies with them. I'll never talk," he declares.

Something tells me his words ring true. I've been workin' the motherfucker over for hours, and he's not said a goddamn word on where Ronan is. *Fuck.*

"Then, so be it," I concede. Giving Gabriel the signal, we all watch as he reveals his blade. "Decirle al diablo que dije hola. *Tell the devil I said hello,*" he says, delivering his parting words as he slits the man's throat. I knew in my gut the man was not going to talk and I wasn't about to waste another minute on his worthless life. Time spent on him was taking away from the time we need to find Lisa.

"Prospect, get this mess cleaned up. Logan, you and Gabriel take care of the body. I'm going to see if Demetri's men came up with any leads."

"You got it, Prez," they say in unison as I make my way up the stairs and out of the basement. Looking at my time, I notice it's after 10:00 pm, and the clubhouse is quiet. Peeking in on Remi, I see her fast asleep in her bed. Closing the door, I go to mine and Grace's room across the hall. Seeing her curled up into a protective ball asleep, I walk past the bed and into the bathroom to take a quick shower. I don't want her to freak out, seeing me covered in blood. Once I'm finished and have changed into some clean clothes, I decide not to wake Grace. Instead, I go to check on Bennett. Opening the door to his room, I'm not surprised to see Emerson sleeping in a chair beside his bed. The sound of the door opening has my brother's head snapping in my direction. The look he is giving me is a silent question, one I don't want to answer. And I don't have to. The look on my face says it all. Bennett and I have known each other our whole lives. When he's hurtin', I'm hurtin'. Without taking his eyes off mine, Bennett says, "Bring my wife home, Jake."

"You have my word, brother."

20

GRACE

Continually checking my rearview mirror, I push my car as fast as it will go. I know as soon as someone realizes I'm missing Jake will lose his shit, but I couldn't stand by and witness another person I've come to care about, be hurt by that monster. Make no mistake, Ronan will kill Lisa. He won't let her go no matter what conditions he wants to be met. My guess is Ronan is going to try and use Lisa to get to me. He'll say he'll want to swap sooner or later, so I am taking matters into my own hands. I won't put Jake in the position to make that decision. Bennett shouldn't have to be without the love of his life because of me. I hope Jake knows how deep my love for him is, and no matter what the outcome, he takes care of my daughter.

My only hope is to get as far away from the compound as I can before Jake or any of the other men catch up with me. When Bennett stumbled in the door with the assistance of Blake, all beaten and bloody with a horrified look on his face as the words that someone took Lisa left his lips, it knocked every ounce of air from my lungs.

Not having a clue as to where they may have taken Lisa, I keep driving. I left everything behind, except for my cell phone. Still having two numbers memorized, I wait another hour before turning off onto a dirt road and drive until I see a farmhouse in the distance before slowing to a stop. Pulling my phone from the back pocket of my jeans, I tap out the first number. After the first attempt goes straight to voicemail, I try the last number I can think of. Ronan's right-hand man, Connor was the one who was always asked to keep a tight rein on my leash when Ronan wasn't around.

On the third ring, the dead tone of his thick Irish accent fills my ear, causing my breath to catch in my throat. "Yeah."

"Connor, put Ronan on the phone," I attempt to tell him, but he cuts me short before I can tell him who I am.

"Who the fuck is this?" Connor barks in a harsh, threatening manner.

Not in the mood to be pushed, I demand through gritted teeth, "Put my husband on the damn phone."

The other end of the line goes silent. I don't even hear his heavy breathing. For what feels like forever, but in reality, it is about two minutes, I hang on the phone in silence.

"Hello, wife." The emotionless baritone of Ronan's voice sends a sharp tingle down my spine. Only in my dreams have I heard that voice for the past two years.

"Cat got your tongue?" Ronan speaks again. This time I can hear the condescending and smirk in his tone.

"You took someone. I want you to let her go, Ronan," I demand.

A sharp bark of laughter pierces through the speaker, causing me to pull the phone from my ear. "What makes you think you are in any position to demand a thing from me, Anna."

Straightening my back, I keep my voice even and firm. "Because I'm willing to trade myself for her. You get me in return if you let her go. You win. You get what you've always wanted, and that's me." Ronan's breath skating across the phone becomes the only noise I hear as I wait for him to reply.

"Where are you? I'll send Connor to get you. Anna, if you are setting me up, she dies, and so do you," he warns.

Before I respond, Connor has been given the phone and starts talking. "Location," he orders.

"Umm," I look around me. "I'm about forty-five minutes east of Polson in a town called Oakdale. Currently, I'm parked on a dirt road just off of Highway 54, called Cooper Lane. I doubt that you will find me, so tell me where to go, and I'll..."

"Stay put," are his final words before the line goes dead.

"Stay put? How the hell do they expect to find me? What am I saying," I shake my head. "this is Ronan I'm talking about." I talk to myself. With nothing more to do but wait, I turn my phone over a few times in my hand, contemplating calling Remi. I'm walking into this knowing I will probably never see her again, and my heart is ripping from my chest thinking about it. Telling myself this is to protect her and to try and save Lisa is doing absolutely nothing to convince me it will work. Knowing Jake and the Club will die protecting her ends up being the knowledge I need to find peace with the choice I have made.

Turning, I glance in the back seat noticing Remi's bookbag. Grabbing the strap, I pull on it and bring it onto my lap and unzip it, looking for paper and something to write with. Finding what I need, I set out to write my daughter a small note. Using the glow of the moon as my light, I put pen to paper.

My beautiful daughter,

I know I don't have to tell you how much I love you because you already know, but I'll say it anyway. I love you, Remi. I'm proud to be your momma and proud to have watched you begin to grow into the young lady you are becoming.

I love you, Peanut.

TEARS STREAM down my cheeks and a couple of them land on the notebook paper, causing two small water stains to soak the edges of the ink. Lifting my hands, I rub them away with the backs of my hands. Sniffling, I look down at the words I wrote to my daughter. On the same piece of paper, I also decided to include a note to Jake.

JAKE,

What can I say? You saw me and showed me what a man's love is supposed to feel like, and I will never let that go. I didn't just survive all those years to protect my daughter. I survived because my forever was waiting for me, and I had to find it—I had to find you. You are my safe place. You are my home. You are my forever.

Keep her safe.

Love you always.

RIPPING the page from the notebook, I hold onto it while tossing the bag and the notebook onto the passenger seat. As I'm folding the letter, a bright beam of lights fills the car and temporarily blinds me as the reflection bounces off the rearview and side mirrors. Shielding the light from my eyes, I turn to try and see the vehicle behind me when knuckles wrapping on my window steals my attention.

Connor's large frame fills the space outside my car door. With his arms crossed, he backs up a few feet and waits for me to open the door. Drawing a deep breath, my hand finds the handle, and I climb out of my car. The note in my hand I crumble to hide in my palm. Feet crunching the gravel causes my head to turn as I take notice of another man walking on the other side of my car holding a large can of gasoline.

A firm hand grips my left arm, and I turn my head toward Connor. He holds his palm out. "Your phone," he demands. Not wanting to provoke him, I comply and hand it over, which he immediately tosses on the hood. The other guy begins to pour gasoline over and around my car then proceeds to throw a match to the ground. Connor leads me toward the SUV they arrived in as the car starts to catch fire. I drop the crumpled note in my hand to the grassy ground before the back door opens, and I climb in. Part of me was expecting to find Ronan sitting in the back seat, but I find no one. In the end, it's Connor, the other guy, and me as they turn the vehicle around and peel off leaving nothing but a fire behind us.

Unfortunately for me, the windows are blacked out to where I can't see my surroundings, so I have no idea which way we are going. Turning his head and looking over his shoulder, Connor looks me over. Raking his beady eyes over my body. A wicked smirk appears on his face as his eyes land on mine, and I give him the best go to hell look I can provide as I press my back to the seat and cross my arms. No words are exchanged. The partition that separates the front from the rear starts to roll up, cutting me off completely, leaving me alone.

I'm not sure how much time has passed when the SUV finally rolls to a stop. At this point, I'm starting to let my nerves get the best of me. All I know is I'm sure by now Jake, and the rest of the club knows I'm gone. I wait for the door to open, and when it does a little light shines on my face causing me to blink and raise my hand to block it. I step out. Glancing around, I try to take in where we are. The house in front of me is an older white colonial style, and we are standing in a circular driveway. There doesn't appear to be anything else around the home, only thick, dense forest as far as I can see through the darkness beyond the well-lit yard. Connor reaches to take hold of my arm, and I take a step to the side preventing his touch, which angers him. His hand shoots out and grabs for my arm again, this time succeeding. Roughly he yanks my small frame into his large one and squeezes my arm to the point of pain.

"That's enough, Connor. Release my wife," Ronan's voice roars. Not breaking the stare off, I continue to shoot daggers at the man holding me.

"I said enough," Ronan bellows once again.

Finally, releasing his tight hold on my upper arm, Connor steps back. I keep my fists balled at my side as I turn my body to face the man I have been running from for two years. I take a good long look at him. Not much has changed. His hair is a little grayer on the top, and he looks to have taken up going to a gym because he isn't as lean as he once was. He has more muscle definition than before.

"Like what you see? Too bad you're not the woman who's been enjoying this body for the past couple of years," he remarks, gesturing to his body with his hands. Ronan has always been full of himself. I cross my arm.

"Trust me. I'm not the least bit envious of any woman you've ever slept with." My words strike a nerve. I watch his smug face warp to one of anger. I insulted him, and I did it in front of his men, something I would have never in a million years done before, but I'm not the woman I was then, and he is taking notice.

"It's going to be fun breaking you all over again, Anna." Giving me his back, Ronan walks inside. Connor takes a step toward me, and this time, I choose to follow Ronan's lead and trail him into the older home. I don't get too far inside the foyer when Ronan spins around. The back of his hand lands a substantial blow to my right cheek, causing my head to snap back. The radiating pain is instant. Finding my center, I stay on my feet and bring my hand to my face covering my throbbing cheek. I won't cower. Dropping my hand, I push my shoulders back and level my stare.

"I see you seem to think you've become a different woman. Stronger even. I'm going to show you just how wrong you are, my dear."

"I can take whatever you dish out, but first let Lisa go. You've got me. She has nothing more to do with this," I demand, even though it's more of a plea. His eyes grow cold.

Stepping into my space and getting right in my face, he continues, "You reek of him, you know that? But you see, my family isn't complete yet. That biker gang still has my daughter, and I want her back. Oh, don't get me wrong, wife. I'm going to have fun with you. I plan on using you up until there is nothing left but your lifeless body. In the end, I'll throw you out like the garbage you are."

A tear rolls down my cheek before I can stop it. I knew I wasn't going to make it out of this alive. The sinking feeling of his words cement the finality of my life, but I'll give my last breath knowing he won't ever get his hands on my daughter. Feeling bold, I spit in his face. "Go fuck yourself. You will never get your filthy hands on **my** daughter." Instead of reacting like I thought he would, which was striking me, Ronan grips the back of my head, grabs a fistful of hair, and forces his mouth over mine. Swiftly, my body gets slammed against the wall, and the struggle to push him off causes him to press his body further into me. Pinning his leg between mine, he makes it a point to press his erection against me. Bringing my hands up, I pull his hair in an attempt to make him stop. Just as quickly, he punches me in the stomach knocking the breath out of me, and I fall to my knees.

"Take her upstairs, " he tells Connor as he looks down on me while I try and catch my breath.

Snatching me from the floor, Connor leads me up the stairs. Stopping in front of the door at the end of the hall, he inserts a key and unlocks the door. Swinging it open, he shoves me inside hard enough I lose my footing and stumble to my knees. The sound of the door slamming shut and locking follows.

"Jesus, Grace," Lisa's voice rings out, and then a pair of arms wrap around my waist as she helps me off the floor, and she settles me on the edge of the bed.

"Lisa, are you okay? Did they hurt you?" Pulling back, I start trying to access her.

"Sweetie, I'm fine. A little banged up from the accident, but other than that, they haven't touched me. My question is, what the hell are you doing here? Where's the men? Oh my God, Grace, please tell me my husband is okay?"

"Bennett is alive. Not in the best of shape, but alive." I lay my hand on her lap and reassure her. "I took off in the middle of the night. I gave myself over to Ronan. To save my daughter and to save you, Lisa," I confess.

The look Lisa gives me is the look I would have gotten from my mother if she were alive. "I can understand doing it for your daughter, but not for me. You should have let Jake and the men handle this mess, Grace. Now look, we are both in the same boat," Lisa informs me of a fact I'm already aware of, but I have a plan.

"Listen, I'm going to need you to follow my lead. I don't know where we are, but we need to try and get out of here." I'm telling her this, and yet I have no intention of running. Getting her out of here is my only concern. "There wasn't much I could see from the outside except trees all around us, but we have to try," I tell her. I walk over to one of the windows in the room and peer out. Lisa joins me.

"What do you suggest we do?" she asks.

Continuing to stare out the window, I state, "We fight."

For what feels like a couple of hours, no one comes into the room, and we both begin to lose a little of the fight we had earlier due to the fact we are both tired. Both our stomachs growl as we continue to walk around the room to stay awake. The sound of the key being inserted into the lock on the other side of the door halts our movements. Grabbing the only thing of use in the room, Lisa stands to where she stays hidden behind the door. I back away a few steps to give myself room to defend myself.

The door opens, and the man that was with Connor earlier appears holding a plate containing two sandwiches. I wait for him to step further into the room before making a move. Lisa pushes the door closed. Raising the lamp above her, she brings it down as hard as she can across the back of his head. Dropping the plate, he stumbles slightly and doubles over grabbing at the back of his injured head. Taking the opportunity just as I see his hand reach inside his jacket, I brace my hands on his shoulders and bring my knee up. The crunching noise I hear lets me know I made solid contact with his nose which brings him down to one knee. Rearing back, Lisa kicks the side of the knee not on the floor, causing it to buckle.

Scrambling, I lock the door as Lisa snatches a drawer from the nightstand. Swinging, the wood cracks across the guy's jaw, knocking him out.

"Holy shit, Lisa," I say in awe.

"Honey, remember who our family is. I picked up some skills of my own along the way," she drops the remaining piece of the drawer to the floor.

"We don't have much time. Does he have keys on him anywhere.?" We begin to search his pockets. Reaching into his suit jacket, my hand grasps his gun. I give it a once over, making sure it's loaded.

"Oh my god," Lisa dangles a set of vehicle keys in her hands.

"Listen, as soon as we break that window, we have to hurry because if this big guy dropping the plate and falling didn't get someone's attention, then glass shattering will. Remember the lattice to the right. We use that to climb down," I rush as we stand in front of the window. Readying ourselves, I use the butt of the gun to break the glass. It doesn't completely shatter, so we use our feet to knock the rest out.

Heavy footsteps echo alerting us to hurry our asses out the window. Lisa climbs out first. I watch over my shoulder with the gun drawn and the safety off ready to shoot whoever crashes through that door.

"Come on," Lisa loudly whispers.

Craning my head out the window, I find her making her way down the side of the house. The door handle jiggling followed by the sound of heavy boots kicking the door fills the room. I turn my head one last time and look at Lisa, who is now on the ground staring back at me.

"No matter what you get in that vehicle, and you keep going." The bedroom door splinters at the hinges. One more kick and I know the only barrier between them and me is coming down. I plead and scream to her one last time. "Lisa, run!"

The door gives way. Raising the heavy gun in my hand, I point and pull the trigger. The bullet rips through Connor's shoulder, but he advances on me before I pull the trigger a second time. The sound of tires spinning the gravel in the distance is the last thing I hear before I take a blow to my face causing my vision to double and my world to go black.

21

JAKE

After another church meeting with my brothers and Demetri, along with his men, I make my way to the kitchen for some much-needed coffee. I'm running on fumes at this point, but none of us have it in us to rest until Lisa is home. So far, we don't have any new leads. Reid was able to tap into some traffic cams and a few security cameras from some local stores but came up with nothing. Demetri's men are headed back out now. Each hour that passes feels like days. Walking into the kitchen, I see Remi sitting at the table drinking what looks like hot chocolate from a mug. Looking down at my watch, I notice it's nearly 3:00 am.

"Hey, sweetheart. What ya doing up?"

"I can't sleep. I hope it's okay that I came down here. Mom usually makes me hot chocolate when I have a hard time sleeping."

"You can have anything ya want darlin'. I'm sure your momma would have made ya some if you had woken her up."

"I was going to, but she's not in her room."

Setting the coffee pot down, I snap my head in Remi's

direction. "What do ya mean she's not in her room. She was in there asleep when I checked on her earlier."

She lightly shrugs one shoulder, "I thought maybe she was with you."

Suddenly, I get a sinking feeling in the pit of my stomach, and I storm out of the kitchen and head straight to my room. I know I won't find her there, though. Bursting through the bedroom door, I take in my empty bed. Next, I look in the bathroom, also nothing. Storming across the hall to Remi's room, I come up with the same thing...no Grace.

Glory, I think to myself, and when I get to her room, I walk in without knocking. My abrupt entrance causes her to stir, and I don't even have it in me to question Demetri as to why he is sittin' in her room watching her sleep.

"Jake, what's going on?" She asks in a sleep filled voice.

"I can't find Grace. Either of you two seen her?" At my question, Glory looks over at Demetri, where he's perched in a chair beside her bed. I don't miss the look on her face that says she had no idea Demetri has been in her room.

"She has to be around here somewhere. I'll help you look," Demetri offers.

"That stupid little shit. I'm going to kill her. I'm going to kill her dead, so help me, Lord. I love her; I love her, but I'm going to murder her," Glory whisper hisses her little rant as she gets out of bed, not shy at all that she's only in a small t-shirt and thong that gives Demetri a clear view of her ass.

"What the hell are you doing?" Demetri growls.

"What the hell does it look like I'm doing. I'm getting my ass out of this bed to get dressed so I can go find my friend and murder her." Glory growls back. Not having time for these two and their tirade, I hold up my hand and bark out, "I want to know what the hell you're talking about, Glory."

"I'm talking about Grace giving us the slip. She's gone to offer herself up to her asshole husband. I knew she was going to pull some shit like this. No way could she live with herself if something happened to Lisa or anyone of you."

"Son of a fuckin' bitch!" I roar, then turn and punch a hole in the wall. My outburst alerting my men because running up the stairs toward us is Logan, Gabriel, Reid, and Quinn. And peaking out from behind Quinn is Remi.

"What the hell, Prez? What's going on?" Logan demands.

"Grace," is all I offer.

"Fuck me," Gabriel grunts.

Walking out from behind Quinn, Remi asks with worry written all over her little face. "Where's my mom?"

"Remi, babe. Come here," Glory coaxes, and Remi runs into her aunt's arms. The kid is smart. She knows. Without another word, I walk out of the room and downstairs with my boys at my back. It's time for some fuckin' heads to roll. If that means I have to tear up this town, and search every goddamn house in Polson, then so be it. And when I get my Little Bird back home, I'm going to tan her ass for this stunt. And Ronan De Burca is going to be wishing for death by the time I get through with him. At the same time, we make it to the main room of the clubhouse; Victor walks in from outside with a stern look on his face.

"What is it, Victor?" Demetri asks from behind me.

"Found Miss Cohen's car on a private road off of Highway 54. It had been set on fire. I found this about thirty feet from what was left of her vehicle. No signs of her inside," he says, handing me a crumpled piece of paper. The words Grace has written on them nearly bring me to my knees. Tucking the paper into the pocket of my cut, I look around me at my boys who are waiting for their President to give them instructions.

"Time to saddle up. It's go time. This shit ends today."

Straddling my bike, I light a cigarette and wait for Quinn to make his rounds with the brothers handing out extra artillery.

When he makes his way to me, he passes me a clip belt along with six loaded clips and two grenades. Raising my eyebrow at him, he shrugs his and says, "Better to be safe than sorry."

A few minutes later, we're all loaded, saddled, and ready to go when Bennett comes limping out of the clubhouse with his arm cupping his side and his head wrapped in a bandage. Emerson is hot on his ass and pissed off.

"What the hell do you think you're doing?" I ask. Not sparing me a glance, he mounts his bike. "I'm going to get my wife. That's what the hell I'm doing. And before you say another word, ask yourself what you would do in my situation. Would you lay your ass in bed, or roll some heads and get your woman back? I heard about Grace, so I already know what your answer would be, brother."

"Fuck, Prez. Can't argue with him there," Quinn cuts in.

Just as I see Emerson about to open her mouth and protest, a big black SUV comes barreling through the front gate and skids to a stop right in front of us, sending dirt and gravel flying everywhere. And before the truck comes to a complete halt, every one of my men is off their bikes and their weapons drawn and pointed directly at the SUV. We are shocked by who we see come flying out of the driver's side door. Lisa.

"Lisa!" Bennett hollers, jumping off his bike, knocking it down in the process, and they run into one another's arms.

"Oh, god! I thought I had lost you," she sobs into Bennett's neck.

"I love you, baby. I love you so much," Bennett tells her in return while holding her face in his hands and peppers kisses on her lips.

After respectfully giving my friends a moment to collect themselves, I come up behind Lisa and place my hand on her shoulder. "I hate to do this now, sweetheart, but time is of the essence. We need to get to Grace. I need you to tell us everything that happened and where Ronan is keeping her."

"Fine, but let's do it on the way there," Lisa tells me as she makes her way over to Nikolai's SUV.

"Where the hell you think you're going, woman?" Bennett snatches her arm, halting her movements.

"To get Grace. And before you try to protest, you best remember I am the only one who knows where they are, and it would be a hell of a lot easier for me to show you than tell you. So, don't bother trying to pull the stubborn alpha card on me, Bennett. Now I suggest we all get our asses in gear and go get Grace."

Without another word, Bennett and I follow Lisa and hitch a ride with Demetri and Victor. We know better than to argue with our momma bear. Before climbing in, I see Logan talkin' to his brother. Nikolai volunteered to stay and watch over the family, along with one of Demetri's men and O'Rourke. Once we pile into the truck, Lisa instructs Victor to turn left out of the compound and head east.

"Lisa, I want you to tell me everything that happened. From the time you were taken up until you got out." She goes on to recount the events from when she and Bennett were run off the road and witnessing him get shot. I can tell by the crack in her voice when saying that part; she truly believed she had lost him.

"You would be so proud of Grace, Jake. All she was concerned about was getting me out of there."

"How were you able to escape?" I ask.

"We kicked one of Ronan's goon's ass, is what we did. When he came into the room we were being held in, I busted a lamp over his head, and Grace kneed him in the face. I am pretty sure she broke his nose too. Once he passed out after I broke a drawer across his face, I found a set of keys in his pocket, and Grace took his gun from the inside of his coat. We broke the window, and she helped me out. Grace didn't have time to follow before someone started trying to kick the door in. She begged me to go—to run. I knew at that point, and so did she, that me making it back to the clubhouse was her only hope. So, I hauled ass to their SUV and got gone, but Jake, there's something else."

"What is it, sweetheart?" I ask, even though I know I don't want to hear the answer.

"Just as I was driving off, I heard a gunshot. I'm sorry, Jake. I didn't want to leave her. I didn't know what else to do. All I could think about was getting to you all as fast as I could," she cries, and Bennett pulls her into his chest.

"You did good, Lisa, and I'm damn proud of ya, you hear. Damn proud."

A few minutes later, we're riding in silence, and the only thing I can hear is the beating of my own heart, and my adrenaline kicks in the closer we get to our destination. Lisa informs us we are about five minutes out of the house Ronan is keeping Grace when Victor pulls off to the side of the road, and my brothers follow suit. The whole scene feels a bit like déjà vu from when Bella and Alba were taken a couple of years ago. With his rifle slung over his shoulder, Reid takes off. He knows the drill. The rest of us men are silent as we ready ourselves. I take a moment to eye each one of my boys. Logan and Gabriel have been in my shoes. They understand what is at stake and that my woman's life is on the line.

"I want to make things clear before we go in. You all do what you have to do to get my girl out of that house, but that motherfucker Ronan is mine," I declare. "Now, let's go in there and show those pussies what happens when you fuck with The Kings."

22

GRACE

When I start to come around, I feel a little disoriented, and my right eye is partially swollen from the blow I took to the face. I'm unable to move my arms. Turning my head, I look to see why. I'm also on my knees, with my arms outstretched, and both wrists are bound with rope to pipes sticking out of the walls on either side of me. With little movement and barely able to see through one eye, I can't get a good look at my surroundings. The lighting is very dim, and it smells a bit musky like mildew. The floor at my knees feels like concrete, which leads me to believe I might be in the basement of the house. Tugging on the ropes causes a burning pain to shoot along my shoulders from the extreme tension in my muscles.

Another thing I notice is how cold I am. Looking down at myself, I realize my clothes are gone. The only article of clothing on my body is my cotton panties. *Oh My God. How long was I out? What else has he done to me?* I close my eyes. Pure panic sets in as I ignore the stabbing pain I'm inflicting on myself by trying to break free. I knew what I was walking into and all the possibilities that came along with my choice to come here, but fear has a way of lurking in the shadows, and right now, it has its claws sunk into my chest.

My thoughts quickly shift to Lisa. I pray she was able to get away. The look on her face when I told her to leave—to run showed the inner struggle she was having with the decision to run and leave me behind or stay, and the fight was hard on her. In the end, her choosing to save herself was what I wanted. If she did make it, I might have a chance at getting out of this alive, because she'll be able to lead Jake and the rest of men back here. *What if she didn't get away? What if she never made it to the vehicle? What if she's dead?* I need to prepare myself for the realization that no one will find me.

The sharp sound of metal against metal breaks through my thoughts and the eerie silence that fills the air, makes me aware of the fact, I am not alone. I do my best to look over my shoulder to see behind me, but the shadows of the room are too dark for me to make anything or anyone.

"I'm impressed. You and that biker bitch took down one of my men. I have to admit I underestimated you, Anna." Ronan speaks from behind me. With the sound of his voice, I freeze. I know this tone. I know it well. The sounds of his shoes clack against the floor with each step he takes, causing a slight echo to bounce off the brick walls as he paces the floor.

"And you shot Connor here." Appearing from the dark corner of the room, Connor slowly strides toward me, holding a gun at his side. Even though I want to show no fear my body betrays me and my breathing picks up. So this is it? This is how my life ends? With a single bullet? "You look a little confused, my dear." Ronan notices I can't take my eyes off the gun. "I'm sure you've heard the saying an eye for an eye, right?"

Connor stops a few feet in front of me, letting his eyes trail my exposed body. Without any hesitation and no time for me to react, he raises the gun and pulls the trigger. In an instant, I scream out in the sheer agony of the pain ripping through my left shoulder just to the side of my collarbone. Blood starts to seep from the gunshot wound and trickles down my side.

"You disappoint me, Anna. You could have had anything you ever wanted. We could have been an unstoppable force. A family bond should never be broken." Stopping beside me, Ronan runs a cold finger along the outer edge of my breast. Bile rises in my throat from his touch.

"Like the way you broke mine? You took my family from me."

Rolling his eyes like I'm some petulant child throwing a tantrum, Ronan huffs an annoyed breath. "This again." He walks away and turns his back toward me for a moment slipping his hands into the pockets of his designer suit pants. "Connor go find out when the helicopter will be here; I need a private moment with my wife," he demands.

"Yes, Sir," Connor responds to the order walking out the door.

Beginning to stroll around me again casually, I wait for his next move. The fire burning in my shoulder is unbelievably intense. Silent tears stream down my face as I do my best to remain motionless against the tautness of the ropes, and the rough, cracked surface of the basement floor beneath me digs into the soft flesh of my knees, almost making that task impossible.

"I know you killed my mother. I don't have proof, but I know you had something to do with the bakery fire. She shouldn't have been there. She never stayed late like that. Not by herself."

Taking his hands from his pockets, he rubs them together. "Unfortunately, your mother did something she shouldn't have. She meddled in affairs that were not her concern. You see, I found out your mother was having me investigated for the murder of your father."

My eyes go wide. Deep in my soul, I knew something wasn't right about the mugging that the cops said took a wrong turn.

Daddy walked the same path home for years. He knew everyone in the neighborhood.

"Your father didn't want me to have you." Ronan stops and cuts his murderous eyes at me, "I always get what I want, Anna." He lifts his lips in a devilish grin. He doesn't have to come right out and say it. The look Ronan gives me is his admission. He killed my father too.

"They both got what they deserved. My family hasn't spent years building an empire for nothing."

"Did you ever love me?" I finally ask. It's not relevant anymore. I stopped loving him years ago, but I want to know if he ever cared for me.

"Love is a strong word to use." He peers up at the ceiling. "I wanted you. I was obsessed with you. My father disapproved of you, and that made me want you more. Then you became a means to an end. I married a sweet, innocent young woman. Someone I could mold," he pauses.

I take a shuddered breath and fight through my pain. "You had plans to force your own daughter into an arranged marriage once she turned eighteen. How could you do something like that? You are a sick bastard. All you ever did was use me, then you planned on using her too. I hate you," I growl.

Ronan gets right in my face. So close, I smell the stench of scotch on his breath. His hand shoots out and takes hold of my chin. "This kind of behavior is unacceptable, Anna, You have to be punished now."

Clenching my teeth, I stare into his cold, menacing eyes. Eyes I once thought held the world. Eyes revealing the monster he is. The old me would beg and plead, but I'm not going to give him the satisfaction. My blank stare and muteness hang between us.

"You were always a screamer. Do you remember? I don't get as much time with you as I had planned," he pushes the hair from my face and tucks it behind my ear, "so we'll have to make this one count. You'll break, Anna. Before I'm done with you, I'll have you begging me to kill you instead." He smirks.

Stepping back, he keeps his eyes trained on mine. I watch him roll the sleeves of his crisp white dress shirt up to his elbows then he begins to undo the buckle on his belt. "Still don't want to ask for my forgiveness?" He laughs.

Defiantly, I raise my chin and hold his stare. I start to lose sight of him as he steps over the rope tied to my right wrist and stands behind me. I stare straight ahead, knowing what comes next.

"Tell me what you did wrong, Anna," he demands of me. My silence is my only answer. The only thing I ever did wrong was love a man like him.

The sharp crack of a leather belt snapping causes my entire body to tense and a lump to catch in my throat. Closing my eyes, I picture the beauty in my life. My daughter, Jake, and my friends, who are my family. I drowned myself in knowing Remi is safe. The first strike of the leather across my skin steals my breath and my back bows. Holding in the scream becomes an act all its own. I won't give him my pain. I won't let him see or have my fear.

"I bet you've been wondering if your friend got away." *Whack whack whack.* The belt hits my flesh several more times. "Beg me to stop," he swings again and again, "and I'll tell you if she got away or if I put a bullet in her head." *Whack.*

It's when the hard end of the buckle splays my back I lose control and wail in pain. He swings the leather, hitting the buckle across my back again and again. "I told you I would break you. I'll have mercy on you and end it all now if you ask me for forgiveness," Ronan rages. *Whack.*

My screams have turned into sobs as he continues his brutal assault. I let my only thoughts be of the ones I love. The images I see when I close my eyes are of all the people who love me.

The basement door flies open, and Connor rushes to say, "The chopper just radioed. They are landing now and said they had eyes on several bikers and some SUVs turning onto the road heading this way, boss. We need to leave. Now."

"Are the explosives set?" Ronan inquiries tossing the belt to the floor.

"Yes, sir," Connor answers back. "We can remote detonate once in the air."

Looking over his shoulder, Ronan gives me one last look. "I won't stop until I have my daughter. Goodbye, Anna."

He's gone. No longer able to hold my weight, I let my shoulders slump. All the pain mingles together, and I sag my head. Muffled voices yell from somewhere outside, and gunfire breaks out. *The Bomb.* If they come into the house, we all die.

23

JAKE

Dust and gravel fly around the truck as we come barreling down the driveway leading to the house Ronan is held up in. It doesn't take long before our presence is known, and bullets begin pinging off the vehicle we are in. My men, knowing Demetri's SUV is bulletproof, they fall in line behind us to dodge being hit. The first thing I notice is how secluded the old abandoned house is. Nothing but trees for miles aside from the large clearing behind the house. And currently landing on that clearing is a fuckin' helicopter. *The fuck?*

Once we have skidded to a stop, Bennett turns to Lisa, who is sitting beside him. "Baby, take this," he says, handing her a Glock. "I want you to stay here and lock the doors behind us. Anybody you don't know comes up to you; you put a bullet in their ass."

Not arguing with his orders, she pulls him to her and lands a hard kiss on his mouth. "Don't get dead."

Demetri, Victor, Bennett, and myself, jump out of the truck and begin rapidly returning fire in the direction of the helicopter where two armed men are perched at the open door with their guns trained on us. There are also three men on the roof of the house. Before any of us has a chance to respond, one by one, all three men slump over and free fall to the ground below. That is when I notice Reid just beyond the tree line to my right. Knowing my brothers have my back, I make my way up to the house. Once I'm stationed at the front door, I give Quinn and Gabriel the signal to circle back on the left side of the house while Demetri and Victor have disappeared around the right corner. With Logan and Bennett covering me, I use my foot and boot in the front door with my gun raised and ready. In quick succession, I put a bullet through the chest of a man in a dark suit who was standing in the living room and quickly pop another two rounds when a couple more fuckers rush around the corner of the kitchen. Suddenly, the house is eerily quiet aside from me hearing the beating of my own heart. Even the sounds of gunfire coming from outside has stopped. All that is left is the hum of the helicopter's propeller blades. With my weapon still raised, I swing my body in every direction scanning the entirety of my surroundings.

"Logan, you and Bennett take the upstairs. I'm going to take a look down here." Without a word, they both nod and head off in the direction of the stairs. Walking down the hallway that leads out of the living room, I come upon an open door that looks like it leads down to a basement and I hear the faint sound of whimpering, and I know it's my Little Bird. My body kicks into motion bounding down the steps two at a time. The closer I get, the louder the cries become, and I clench my jaw and try to prepare myself for what I may find. Clearing the last step with my gun raised in the air, I try to take in the room. It's so dark the only thing I see is a shadowy figure crouched on the floor. Just then, Bennett appears behind me flashing his cell phone light. When the room is illuminated, I am not at all prepared for the sight in front of me. My woman is on her knees, slumped over, and she has her arms pulled out to her sides by fuckin' ropes. With a roar escaping my mouth, I drop to my knees next to Grace.

"Bennett, I need that light over here. I can't see shit, and I need to cut these fuckin' ropes." When he trains the light on Grace, my blood turns cold at what I see. "Son of a bitch," I growl, and Bennett wastes no time checking the bullet hole in her shoulder.

"It's a clean shot."

Not only has my woman been shot, but her back is black and blue and has welts that I know has been caused by the motherfucker's belt. "Baby," I speak gently. "I'm going to cut these ropes, okay?" I tell her, and when my hand touches her arm, she flinches from the pain of being touched. It's also then I feel how cold her skin is. Grace is in nothing but a pair of panties. My mind starts to wonder what else Ronan has done to her, and suddenly my own body is vibrating in anger.

"You need to get out of the house," Grace rasps out. "You have to hurry, Jake. Please."

"Everything is going to be okay, baby. I'm going to get you out of here," I assure her while using my knife to cut the ropes.

"Bomb," she says before she passes out. *Fuck!*

"Did she just say bomb?" Bennett asks.

"Shit! We have to hurry, brother." Just as I finish cutting the last rope, Logan comes charging down the stairs.

"The fuckin' pussy got away, Prez." His words are cut off when he sees the state Grace is in.

"Son of a fuckin' bitch," Logan hisses through clenched teeth.

Scooping Grace up into my arms as carefully as possible, I hold her naked body close to me, shielding her as much as possible. "We need to move now! Grace said there was a bomb in the house. Go! Go! Go!" I shout. When the three of us clear the basement, we are met with Quinn and Gabriel walking in from outside. "Out now!" The urgency in my voice has my men not wasting any time running out the door. We barely make it off the steps of the porch when there is an explosion, and I can feel the heat on my back as the force of the bomb brings me to my knees with Grace still in my arms. Thank fuck Grace is still passed out. It's also then that I realize my boys, Logan, Gabriel, Reid, and Quinn, have used their bodies to shield Grace and me by forming a circle around us.

I'm picking myself up off the ground, and quickly stride toward Demetri's truck when Lisa jumps out of the back seat of the SUV with her pistol raised and fires off a single shot just over my left shoulder. Momentarily stunned, I look over my shoulder and see one of Ronan's men lying on the ground about twenty feet behind us with a bullet between his eyes.

"Let's go!" Lisa orders, and without another word, I file into the truck behind her as my brothers mount their bikes and we hall ass.

"Hospital?" Victor asks from the driver's seat.

"No. Hospital means cops. No way am I dealing with that shit and handing Ronan over to them. He's mine."

I look at Bennett, "You said the shot in her shoulder was clean. Does she need a hospital?"

"No. I'm going to call Emerson and make sure she has the supplies we'll need once we get back to the clubhouse."

"Jake?" Grace croaks interrupting us.

"I got you, Little Bird. I got you." Stroking her hair, I try soothing her.

"I'm so cold." Grace begins to shiver in my arms.

"Shit! Lisa, look in the back for something to cover her up with."

Reaching into the very back, Lisa shuffles around and comes back with a small blanket. "Here ya go, Jake."

Using the blanket, I try carefully to tuck it around her without jostling her too much. Every little movement I make causes her to wince in pain. Even her eyes are so swollen she can hardly open them.

"Lisa, babe. Hand me my medic bag from back there too," Bennett tells his wife. Passing him his bag, he unzips it and produces a needle and a vile. At my questioning look, he mutters, "Something to help her sleep. We have about a forty-five-minute drive. No need for her to suffer if she doesn't have to." Thank god he doesn't go anywhere without being prepared.

When we arrive back at the clubhouse, Emerson is already waiting for us outside when we pull up. When I step out of the SUV with Grace in my arms, she doesn't ask any questions as she follows behind me into the clubhouse up the stairs and down the hall to my room. I called ahead of time to make sure Remi would be preoccupied somewhere else upon our arrival. She doesn't need to see her momma in her current condition. Walking into my room, I carefully deposit Grace down on the bed, and Emerson immediately gets to work assessing her. A few seconds later, Glory comes bursting in. When she gets her first glimpse of Grace, she breaks out into a sob and covers her mouth with her hand. Quickly pulling her shit together, she squares her shoulders and asks, "Emerson, what do you need me to do?" Emerson starts to bark out orders at Glory and she wastes no time jumping into motion. When I see Lisa walk in the room, I stride over to her and put my hands on her shoulder.

"We got things covered in here, sweetheart. Be with your old man. You both have had a helluva twenty-four hours, and right now, he needs you and you need him." Lisa is about to protest when I cut her off. "I know the momma bear in you wants to help, but right now being a wife comes first. Now go," I urge and kiss the top of her head.

An hour later, Emerson has stitched the gunshot wound, and

she and Glory have given Grace a sponge bath to clean off all the blood. Emerson also puts cream on her back and assured it would help with the pain and healing of the lashes caused by the belt. Glory has been periodically placing ice-packs on Grace's face to help with the swelling around her eyes. Through all this, she has yet to wake up from the shot Bennett gave her in the truck. Now we wait. Thankfully we don't have to wait long because another twenty minutes later, Grace begins to stir. Her movements have me, Emerson, and Glory by her side in seconds.

"Jake?"

"I'm here, Little Bird?" I say, taking her hand in mine and bringing it to my lips.

"Where am I?"

"You're at the clubhouse. Emerson is here, and so is Glory."

"How bad is it?" she asks, and I know she's referring to her injuries.

"What do you remember, baby?"

"Everything," she sighs breathlessly. "Besides the ride home, I remember everything."

When I see silent tears fall down her swollen cheeks, I wish with everything I am that I could take away the memory and pain of what that sick motherfucker did to her.

"He didn't break me this time. He tried. He wanted me to break so bad, but I didn't. I'd rather die than have him take back what I fought so hard to get."

"I'm so proud of you, baby." I choke past my own emotions while Emerson and Glory are no longer able to hold theirs back, and they both quietly sob. Wiping her tears away, Emerson transforms back into doctor mode when she asks a question I dreaded but knew it was coming. "Grace, I need to ask you a question."

"Okay."

Releasing a deep sigh, she asks, "Were you raped? When you

arrived here at the clubhouse, you didn't have any clothes besides your panties. When I removed them to clean you up and put fresh clothes on, you had a small amount of blood in them. I did not examine you. I wouldn't do so without your consent."

Grace stares at Emerson for a beat like she's trying to put the past events together. "I...I don't know."

24

GRACE

When Emerson asks the question that had popped into my head moments after I came to and found myself bound and most of my clothes gone, I wish I could have instantly said no. The truth is any number of things could have happened while I was knocked out. At the moment, the throbbing and piercing pain radiating from my back and my shoulder are the only focal points registering. My eyes shift to Jake who has stood stock still this whole time. If possible, the man before me grows taller, and he starts to pace the floor with his fists clenched at his sides doing his best to hold in the building anger written all over his handsome face. And it guts me.

I give my attention back to Emerson. "I don't think so, but I can't give you a definite no," I tell her. My mouth feeling dry, I try reaching for the small glass of water sitting on the bedside table. Emerson helps by handing it to me. Slowly I sip through the straw and wet my dry, scratchy throat.

"When I get my hands on that motherfucker I'm going to make his death slow and torturous," Jake growls then proceeds to put his fist through the wall beside the bedroom door. Seconds after there's a sharp, hard knock on the door. Jake rips it open, damn near pulling it from its hinges and answers with a harsh, "What?"

Calmly standing in the hallway is Logan, utterly unfazed by Jake's rage. Glory comes to sit beside me on the bed. Taking my hand in hers, she comforts me as I watch Logan talk to Jake in hushed tones. Jake eventually gives him a firm nod, then pivots, making his way to my side. "Babe," he lets out a heavy sigh and closes his weary eyes. Opening them, he settles his loving eyes on mine. "I'll be downstairs with the men. I promise I'm not going anywhere. As soon as Emerson finishes with her examination, someone will get me. This is the only time I'll be leaving your side tonight, Little Bird." Leaning forward Jake kisses my forehead before softly pressing his lips against mine, letting himself linger there for a second longer before standing and leaving the room.

Pulling in a deep breath, I silently thank Logan for showing up when he did.

"Honey, it's okay that you can't remember. Is there a possibility you've started your cycle?" Emerson asks.

I try to remember what today's date is so I can give her an accurate answer. It's then I realize I'm past my cycle date.

"Grace, is there a possibility you're pregnant?" Glory gasps.

I continue to stay lost in thought. We haven't used any protection since the first time Jake and I made love. Holy shit. I could be pregnant. I lick my lips, suddenly feeling very thirsty again. I look from Glory to Emerson, both eagerly waiting for my reply. "Can you do a pregnancy test? Today?" I ask Emerson.

"We can do that. I want to be sure, so let's draw some blood, and I'll take it to the lab myself. One of the techs there owes me a favor, so I'll get a great turnaround time," she explains as she preps my arm to take some of my blood.

"If you are comfortable with me doing it, I can go ahead and examine you right here once I'm done with the bloodwork," Emerson explains.

"Yes. I need to know."

After walking to the bathroom to wash her hands, Emerson comes back and finishes prepping herself and me. The examination, although a little uncomfortable, was over as quickly as it started.

With a reassuring smile, she tells me, "I saw no signs of trauma that would suggest any forced penetration. I don't believe there was any sexual assault. So, I'm going to run to the hospital. I shouldn't be gone but a couple of hours tops."

Shifting to find a better position in the bed, I lay on my side. "This is crazy," I remark. I could be carrying Jake's baby, and nothing about the thought scares me. If anything, it makes me happier than I can imagine. It makes me love him even more. It also makes me think about my parents.

"I'll see you in a little while, Grace. Take a couple of these for the pain." She hands me some over the counter pain medication. "I won't prescribe anything stronger until we get the results back. In the meantime, try to rest." Slipping her bag over her shoulder, Emerson slips out the door, leaving only Glory and myself in the room.

"He killed them, Glory. My parents. He killed both of them." The weight of everything starts to catch up with me, and I cry. Not for myself, but for my parents. They did nothing but love me and want the best for me, and he took them from me for that very reason. Stretching out beside me, so we are laying face to face, my best friend holds my hand.

"They still walk beside you, Anna, and they are so proud of you, honey." She squeezes my hand. She's right. I feel them with me every day.

"You want me to go get Jake?" Glory questions.

"Stay just a little while longer. Maybe you could sing to me? I haven't gotten to hear you sing in a long time," I smile, remembering all the times we sang some of our favorite songs while using our hairbrush as a microphone. Our only audience was each other. I never could carry a tune, but Glory has a soft angelic voice. When she sings, it has this way of soothing the soul. You feel it bone deep. She smiles, and I close my eyes and wait. When she starts to sing *The Scientist* by Coldplay, I lose myself in the soothing, fluid sounds of her voice.

SOMETIME LATER, I wake to feel rested. Blinking sleep from my eyes, I notice Glory is no longer next to me. With slow movements, I roll onto my back and start to push my body upwards to sit against the headboard when I feel Jake's arm snake around my middle. Placing my hand on his, I turn my head and look beside me. "Hey," I smile down at him as he watches me.

He clears his throat, then shifts, placing his head onto my lap. "You were sound asleep when I came back up so I laid beside you the best I could with touching you. I must have fallen asleep. How are you feeling?"

"Much better now that I'm home, and you're beside me." Raising my hand, I run my fingers through his hair. He looks exhausted. "I love you, Jake."

My soothing touch causes his eyes to close as I continue to stroke his hair. "And I live and breathe for you." He releases on an exhale, which brings a smile to my face. "Where's Remi?" I softly ask.

"With Glory. Would you like for me to go get her, babe?" Pushing himself up, he sits against the headboard as well but keeps contact with me by holding my hand in his.

"Please," I reply. I'm sure by now, my daughter has attempted several times to check on me. Leaning across the bed, Jake cradles my face in the palm of his hand and lowers his lips to mine. "I love you so much, Grace." Lightly burying his face into the crook of my neck, we have a moment. A moment to appreciate each other. A moment to be thankful.

Climbing out of bed, Jake walks out of the room and quickly returns with a visibly upset Remi. Opening my arms, she jumps on the bed and tucks herself into my side and lays her head against my uninjured shoulder and starts to do something she doesn't often do—cry. Remi is not a crier. Never has been. So for her to be this upset, it rips at my heart. "Shh, Peanut," I rub her arm and hold her tight. She doesn't speak. My daughter is my whole world. I lift my eyes to Jake, who is standing by the door. I motion for him to join us by patting the mattress with my hand. Sliding himself close to my other side, Jake raises his arm, and I carefully tuck myself into his side as he protectively holds me as I embrace my daughter—As he embraces his family.

A few minutes later, someone knocks on the door. "Come in," Jake announces not wanting to budge. Emerson pokes her head in and peeks before fully stepping inside ."Oh, would you like me to come back a little later?" she asks her question directed at Jake.

"No, come on in, sweetheart," Jake assures her. She places a small bag on the dresser beside the bedroom door. "I have the results from the blood work," she looks directly at me. A knowing smile passes between us, giving me the answer I've been waiting for. Tucking a strand of hair behind her ear, she digs into her bag and produces what looks like a small computer. Attached to it is what looks like one of those ultrasound wands they use in a doctor's office.

"If you can, Grace, would you scoot down and lay flat on your back for me?" Emerson instructs me while she flips open the computer top.

"Mom, are you going to be okay?" Remi questions and moves over to allow me to lay back. "Yes, Peanut. I'm going to be okay," I assure her. Jake assists me by adding a second pillow under my head for more comfort. At this point, the only time my back hurts is when my movement pulls at the skin, but it's not as painful as it was several hours ago.

"Is someone gonna tell me what we are looking for?" Jake demands.

"This is a portable ultrasound. It's going to allow me to see images of the inside." Lifting my shirt to expose my stomach, she starts spreading the jelly on my lower abdomen. Emerson glides the ultrasound wand back and forth and applies a little firm pressure as she does it.

"And what are you looking for," Jake questions her again, his eyes fixed on the small screen.

I hold my breath.

"I'm looking for..." Emerson says slowly as she moves to another spot, "there," she stops. Emerson taps a key on the computer, and the sound becomes louder.

Whoosh, whoosh, whoosh.

Remi gasps beside me but doesn't say a word as her face lights up for the first time in days. I look to Jake, who's wearing a shocked expression on his face. Dragging his hand through his beard, Jake asks her, "Is that what I think it is?"

"That, guys, is your baby's heartbeat, and that right there," she points to a tiny blip on the screen, "is your baby. You are, in fact, pregnant. Now, I won't 100% say how far along you are but by the look of things, I would guess eight weeks." Emerson lets us listen to the rhythm of the fast heartbeat a moment longer before setting the wand aside and cleaning the sticky jelly from my skin. "Everything looks good. First thing tomorrow, find an OBGYN and set up an appointment. Congratulations, guys! I'm beyond happy for all three of you."

"Momma, you're going to have a baby. Oh my gosh, I'm going to be a big sister. This is unbelievable," Remi gushes with excitement. "Please, please can I go tell Aunt Glory, I'm about to burst," she quickly stands and starts bouncing.

By this point, I've started crying again, only this time they are happy tears. "Yes, Peanut, you can go tell her." Before the words finish leaving my mouth, she's darting to the bedroom door but stops just as she's about to put her hand on the door handle.

Spinning around, she makes a beeline toward Jake and throws her arms around his neck. "Thank you," she whispers. Visibly overcome, I watch Jake struggle to hold his emotions in check until Remi runs out the door, and Emerson quietly follows, closing the door behind her.

"You know we have maybe thirty seconds before my best friend comes bursting through that door?" I laugh.

Jake remains quiet as he eases his body down the bed until his face hovers over my still exposed belly. The warmth of his breath brushes across my skin just before he kisses it. I listen to his shuddered breaths as he attempts to rein them in.

"I'm not sure how to put into words what I'm feeling right now. I feel like nothing I say would do justice to the immense joy and love I have for you at this moment," his voice cracks with emotions.

"You don't have to say anything. You've shown me—you've proven time and time again; you love me; love us. That is all I will ever need from you, Jake."

25

JAKE

Wanting to give Grace some alone time with Remi and Glory, I decide to head out to the main room for a beer and see what my brothers are up to. My focus the past twenty-four hours has been solely on my woman, yet I know my boys have been working endlessly on tracking down Ronan. It chaps my ass that the slimy bastard slipped through our fingers. *Fuckin' pussy.* But not even the fact that fucker got away can overshadow the news that I'm going to be a dad. My Little Bird is going to have my baby. Suddenly, a dark shadow crosses my heart because for the first time since hearing the news, I realize not only could I have lost Grace, but I could have lost my baby. It's a miracle the baby survived the beating she had to endure by that pussy Ronan.

I look forward to having his blood on my hands. Saddling up to the bar, I take a seat next to Logan and motion for the prospect Grey to give me a beer. Lifting the bottle to my mouth, I down half the contents in one pull.

"How's Grace doing?" Logan asks from beside me.

At his question, I turn and look at him, and the rest of the men I consider my sons. Gabriel, Reid, Quinn, and I smile.

"Grace and I are going to have a baby," I say, dropping the bomb. Maybe I should have waited longer, but I'm so fuckin' ecstatic. Plus, with all the shit going on it feels good to deliver a piece of good news.

Choking on his drink, Quinn spits out. "No fuckin' way! Are you yankin' our chain, Prez?"

"Nope, Emerson just confirmed."

A round of whoops and congratulations echoed throughout the room.

"I'm so damn happy for ya, Prez," Logan says, clapping me on the back. "You fuckin' deserve this," he mutters pulling me in for a hug.

"Thanks, son."

After a beat of silence. Quinn's ass doesn't disappoint when he speaks up. "I can't believe Jake's old ass is gonna be a daddy before me."

"Fuck you, Quinn." I chuckle, throwing my bottle cap at him the same time Gabriel slaps him upside his head.

"What! I'm just sayin'. All of y'all are havin' babies. I can't wait to have a whole fuckin' litter. Now, if my baby momma would get her ass on board."

"Let me give you a piece of advice, Quinn," Emerson interjects, walking into the room and takes a seat at the bar to my left. "Don't refer to your future children as a litter."

"No problem, babe. I'll leave the name pickin' to you."

Rolling her eyes, Emerson ignores Quinn, as hard as it is at times, and turns her attention to me. "I see you told them your happy news."

"Shit, doc. I couldn't keep something like that in. Still can't fuckin' believe it. I know we probably should have waited a little longer before announcing—" I go to say, but Emerson cuts me off.

"With all this club is going through right now, I think a little good news is warranted. This is your family, Jake. Share this happy time with them. And like I said before, Grace is doing well considering, and the baby's heartbeat is strong. For now, don't think about the what-ifs. The what-ifs are irrelevant."

"You're right, doc. Thanks."

"Mind if I stay and have a beer? Or are you all having some sort of meeting?"

"No, sweetheart. Stay." Lifting a finger to Grey. "Get Emerson a beer."

"You got it, Prez."

"Anyone know where the hell my father and brother went. I haven't seen their asses since we got back?" Logan grills. And come to think of it he's right. I have not seen either Demetri or Nikolai since we rolled back up at the clubhouse. I've been so focused on Grace; I haven't noticed their presence was missing.

"Haven't seen them, brother," Gabriel gruffs. "Victor is MIA too."

No sooner does Gabriel get those words out when the door to the clubhouse slams open and causes myself and my brothers to move into action. Pulling my piece from my cut, I swiftly shove Emerson behind me and point my gun at who just walked through my door. It takes but a second to realize it's Demetri, Nikolai, and Victor. All three look a little worse for wear. But that is not what has my hackles rising, and Logan rushing to his father's side is the fact that Demetri was shot.

"What the fuck happened to you?" I bark. "Emerson! We need you again."

"Jesus Christ! I might as well start my own practice because this club keeps me busier than the damn hospital," she smarts off, rushing to Demetri's side.

Looking relaxed as ever, Demetri replies. "It's just a flesh wound—no big deal. Besides, the result was well worth it," he smirks.

"Hey, Jake? Anna wanted..." Glory starts to say, walking into the room, then comes to a complete stop with the sight in front of her. "Is this sort of thing normal around here?" she gestures with a raised eyebrow to Demetri's bleeding arm.

"Is Grace alright?" I question.

"Yeah, yeah, she's fine. I'll just tell her you're a bit indisposed at the moment."

Before I have a chance to say more, Glory turns on her heel and leaves the room. Blowing out a frustrated breath, I shift my attention back to the scene in front of me. Demetri is now sitting on a stool by the bar and downs a shot of whiskey while Emerson takes a look at his wound. I take a moment to size up Nikolai as well. He doesn't appear to be hurt, but gone is his standard attire of tattered jeans and work boots. Right now, Nikolai looks much like his father in his Armani suit and peeking out from the inside of his suit jacket is two pistols strapped to his holster.

"He's right," she says. "Just a simple flesh wound. It looks like the bullet only grazed his arm. He'll need a couple of stitches, though. Let me get some supplies. I'll be right back."

"Now, with that shit out of the way, you want to tell me where you, Nikolai and Victor have been the past twenty-four hours? And why after being MIA, you suddenly show up here looking like shit?"

"As you all know, family means everything to me. I consider every one of you, my family. I did what was necessary to protect my family," Demetri states. Straightening in his seat, Demetri's face and tone becoming more serious. "Son?" Demetri addresses Nikolai giving him a look. Nikolai then strides over to the edge of the room next to the hallway blocking the entrance. Now my senses are on high alert.

"Victor." Demetri nods to his right hand, who is standing guard at the front entrance. When Victor opens the door, another one of Demetri's men walks in with a man's body slumped over his shoulder. Making his way over to me, the man tosses the body to the floor in front of me with a thud. Laying on the floor at my feet is none-other than Ronan De Burca.

"I saved one for you, my friend," Demetri delivers.

Looking down at this pathetic excuse of a man, a wicked smile takes over my face. "Who's up for a little retribution?"

"Hell, fuckin' yeah!" Quinn cheers and the rest of the men follow suit.

"Gabriel, take his ass down to the basement. I'll be down in a minute."

Stepping up to Demetri, I offer my hand. "I owe ya one, brother."

"No, you don't. This is what family does. We have each other's back. You and your club have accepted Nikolai and me into your fold, and you helped me get my son back. It is me who owes you," he finishes shaking my hand.

Before I take care of business, I go to check on Grace since Glory never did finish telling me what she needed. When I walk into our room, I smile when I see her sitting up in bed and eating with Glory and Remi at her side.

"Can I have a minute alone with Grace?" I ask them.

"Sure," Glory agrees, taking Remi's hand and leading her out of the room then shutting the door behind them.

"Jake, is everything alright?"

"Yes, but I have something I need to tell you." Kneeling on the floor next to the bed, I take Grace's battered face in my hands and kiss her busted lips. "I love you, Little Bird."

"I love you too, Jake. Now tell me what's going on."

"I want you to know that it's over. You don't have to worry about the De Burcas' anymore."

"What exactly do you mean?" she exhales a shaky breath. "Can you be more specific?"

"I mean, Demetri went to Chicago and ended them?"

"And Ronan?"

"Ronan was brought here." At my confession, Grace's body stiffens.

"You have nothing to be afraid of, babe. Demetri knew Ronan's life was mine. That's why he was brought here."

Grace is silent for a few beats before she speaks again. Looking me dead in my eyes, she orders with a cold tone. "I want you to do to him what he's done to me. I want him to suffer."

The moment I open the door to the basement, Ronan's angry voice echoes off the walls. "You won't get away with this! My men will end every one of you. You low-life bikers are going to regret this!" With a menacing chuckle, I clear the last step and walk fully into the room. Gabriel has Ronan strung up by his wrists, and he has been stripped down naked. Meanwhile, Logan, Reid, Quinn, and Bennett stand around, looking bored.

"Nobody will be coming for you, you cocksucker, because they are all dead. Your father included," I deliver the bad news. At first, he looks like he doesn't believe me, but then he looks around at the smug look on my men's faces, and he suddenly pales. The look doesn't last long before he quickly recovers, and his arrogance is showing again.

"You sure are going through a lot of trouble for my whore of a wife."

Not two seconds after those words leave his mouth, I bring my booted foot up and swiftly nail him in the balls. Ronan screams out like a little girl and vomits onto the basement floor. My action causes the men in the room to groan and wince. "With a dick that little, any woman who has the displeasure of sleeping with you is going to eventually look for a man with a cock that can satisfy them. And don't worry, Grace is plenty satisfied."

Striding to the far-right corner of the basement, I pick up the water hose and make my way back to the piece of shit who is making a mess on my floor. Turning it on, I proceed to douse Ronan's body with icy cold water. Fifteen minutes later, he is a shivering pathetic mess. Dropping the hose, I walk up to Ronan and get in his face. "You want to know what Grace requested right before I came down here? She told me to make sure I do to you what you've done to her. To make you suffer the way she did. And you know what? Nothing will bring me more pleasure than doing just that," I tell him as I step back and proceed to unbuckle my belt and slip it off. "I even wore the one belt with the biggest fuckin' buckle, just for you." This is the first time my brothers are getting a notion of what Grace's husband has done to her. And I see the fury in their eyes as they put two and two together as I remove my belt from around my waist. They knew she endured some abuse, but I never disclosed what kind. I know that what is said in this basement will never make it beyond these walls. Grace will never have to worry about them knowing because they will never say a word.

With my belt tightly gripped in my hand, I circle my prey. "Only a pussy would put their hands on a woman. Only a cocksucker would take his belt and beat a woman in an attempt to break her. Only a little dick son of a bitch feels he has to make a woman feel less than him," I spit, and in one swift swing, I deliver my first lash across Ronan's back, causing him to bow. *Whack, whack, whack.* My belt makes contact three more times and each one of my swings becomes more forceful. The images of Grace's scars are at the forefront of my mind, and the memory of finding her naked body tied up in that house is fueling my rage. I continue to swing until my arm is tired and I lose count as to how many blows I have given, and Ronan's screams of pain vibrate off the walls.

Taking a few steps back, I look at the defeated bloody piece of shit before me. "You don't have shit to say anymore, do ya? How about asking for mercy? That's what I want. Ask me for mercy and to forgive you, just like you demanded of my woman."

"The bitch deserved everything she got," Ronan bites out

through the pain. Taking my gun from my cut, I aim it and fire a single shot to his shoulder. The same shoulder Grace was shot in. With Ronan roaring out in pain, I rush up to the fucker, grab a fist full of his hair, and force his steely eyes to look at me. "That bullet was for Grace. The same woman who you did not break. The same woman who is upstairs in my bed with my baby in her belly and my daughter at her side. That's right motherfucker, Remi is my daughter now."

Releasing his head, I step back, and motion to Bennett who steps forward without a word raises his piece and fires a bullet into Ronan's ribs. "That's for my wife and me," he seethes and spits at Ronan's feet.

"What do you think of us low-life bikers now? How does it feel knowing that your whole empire was brought down by the Volkovs and The Kings? Better yet, how does it feel knowing you'll be burning in hell, while Grace will become my queen? And do you want to know somethin' about my queen? She doesn't ask anyone for forgiveness. Nor does she ask for mercy. Because now Grace takes what she wants. In your case, it will be your pathetic life. And what my queen can't take; I take for her." With those parting words, I raise my pistol and fire one last shot, right between Ronan's eyes.

26

GRACE

Stretching my arms over my head, I open my eyes. The morning sun has started to bask the bedroom with its warmth and light making it a perfect start to a beautiful Montana day. I can not believe how much our lives have changed. Ronan and his family are gone. They are no longer a shadow looming over our lives, and I no longer have to run or hide. There are so many wonderful people in my life to thank for the fact we are free of worry. Waking up every morning for the past few weeks finally able to breathe a sigh of relief that we have been able to go about our day to day without having to look over our shoulder is our new reality now, and I'm beyond thankful. Remi has gone back to school, I've been working at the bakery every day, and Jake has been able to focus on the rebuilding of his shop.

"Come here," Jake rumbles, his voice raspy from sleep as he pulls my body close to his.

"Morning," I softly say and run my fingers through his beard.

"What are your plans for the day, babe," he asks, palming my left breast.

"The usual. Dropping Remi off at school, going to work."

Leaning in close, his warm breath causes goosebumps to spread across my flesh as he drags his lips down my neck, then across my shoulder. I lose concentration when Jake gently rolls one nipple between his thumb and forefinger and takes the other into his mouth. My hands begin to explore his bare chest, back, and strong arms as he brings his massive body to hover over mine. My legs open letting him settle between them and his thick, heavy arousal presses against my inner thigh.

"I've barely touched you, and your pussy is hot for me." Jake moans, and I continue to press against him. "You are so fuckin' beautiful, Little Bird," he tells me before stealing my breath with an all-consuming kiss as his lips claim mine. His hand skates down my side and over the flare of my hip as he lowers himself. Wrapping his fingers behind my knee, he guides my leg to rest on his shoulder. Feeling bold, I reach between us and wrap my small hand around his girth giving him a few strokes. "Fuck, babe, do that again," his eyes close. I stroke him a few more times. "Keep your hand wrapped around my cock and guide me into that sweet pussy, Little Bird," he demands. Pulling back, Jake pauses. With my leg still draped over his shoulder, he slowly sinks into me. Taking his time Jake's movements are slow as he makes love to me.

"More, Jake," I beg.

"I. Will. Never. Get. My. Fill. Of. You. Grace. Never." He grunts with every thrust. Bearing down, Jake's pelvic bone makes perfect contact with my swollen clit sending me over the edge. My orgasm so intense my back bows, and I moan out his name. At the same time, he growls "Fuck," as he finds his release with me.

Resting my palm on Jake's cheek, I gaze into his eyes. "I still can't believe you're mine," I whisper.

"I'm the lucky one, Grace," he replies.

. . .

LATER IN THE DAY, I close the bakery to meet Glory for some lunch. "Have you been in touch with your parents yet?" I ask Glory who is sitting across the table from me while we wait for Finn to show. He called this morning and asked us to meet him this afternoon.

"I called them last night," she picks the menu up and glances over it as she continues. "I told them you're having a baby, and now my mother is harping on me about giving her a grandchild," she gives a quick pause accompanied by a smile, "so thanks for that," she teases. Glory is over the moon, happy for us. It didn't take long before she practically knocked the door down on the day we found out after Remi ran off to tell her. Since then, not only do I have Jake shadowing my every move, my best friend has begun doing the same.

Laughing off her mother's eagerness to be a grandma, I try to decide between the Cobb salad or caving to my cravings and order the double bacon chili cheeseburger. Catching notice of Finn walking through the door, I wave at him to grab his attention and he strides in our direction toward the back corner of the small restaurant where Glory and I are seated.

"I appreciate the time, ladies," Finn greets with a smile and pulls a chair from the adjacent table and joins us. In his hand is a folder and he hands it to me and clears his throat. "As you are aware, Ronan didn't have any more family besides his father. All remaining relatives were distant cousins. Since you were legally still married to him, by default, all his assets go to you and Remi." As he is explaining all this to me, I open the folder and thumb through tons of papers and legal documents stunned by what I'm hearing. "You'll find that many assets liquidated due to some back taxes owed to the government, but you were left with a good chunk of money."

I glance at Glory. She knows what I'm thinking. Putting the papers back into the folder, I slide it back toward Finn. "I don't want his dirty money."

Just as quickly, Glory snatches the folder before Finn reaches for it. "Wait, how much money are we talking about here," she says and peeks through to find the seven-figure number among the pages. "Grace, honey. Maybe you need to think about this. You deserve this money. That bastard put you through hell. Take the money."

"No," I clarify. Glory gives me another 'are you sure' look before letting it go.

"What do you suggest to be done with this money then, Grace?" Finn asks. The waitress walks up. We order lunch, and as we wait, I think about how I can use the money for good. When I look back to Finn, I know what I want to do. I want to help others. Grabbing the folder, I tuck it away in my shoulder bag. "We donate it." I smile, knowing who I'll be making the check out to.

"So, Finn, what are your plans? Are you going back to the city?" Glory changes the subject just as our food arrives.

"I'll be leaving tomorrow. A new undercover assignment was offered, and I'm taking it," Finn tells us.

"So this lunch is also your goodbye," I state.

"For now," Finn says. "I'll check in from time to time. I happen to like this town and the people in it, so you'll see me again."

Trying not to let my emotions get the best of me, I tell him, "There is nothing I could ever do to repay you for everything you've done for me and my daughter, Finn. You saved us."

"I may have helped, but you saved yourself, Grace." He says full of pride.

I'M CURRENTLY ENJOYING a cup of decaffeinated coffee curled up with a light throw blanket draped across my legs on the back porch swing as I watch Jake and Remi feed the horses apples.

Two days ago, Jake surprised Remi with the fact he bought the two horses she's been attached to the moment we arrived out here weeks ago.

I take another sip of my coffee. The light breeze carries the smell of rain of the distant storm clouds, and I can see Remi bounding up the porch steps. "I'm going to go pack my overnight bag," she stops long enough to give me a quick hug before disappearing inside. She and Kat have become the best of friends since meeting at the clubhouse during the threat and have been inseparable since. So, on our way to Bella's house today we'll be stopping at Victoria and Quentin's house.

When Jake makes it to the porch, he leans down, kissing me. "Hey, beautiful."

"You spoil her too much," I jest, with a hint of seriousness. Setting my mug down, I throw the blanket across the back of the swing and stand.

Tucking me into his side, we make our way indoors just as thunder rumbles in the distance. "Get used to it, Little Bird. I plan on giving you, Remi," Jake places his hand protectively over my stomach, "and our baby in your belly everything I can give."

"All we need is you and your love, Jake," I admit.

A couple of hours later, we've dropped Remi off, and Jake has just dropped me off at Bella's house while he and the guys meet with the insurance adjuster in town about the garage. All the ladies are here today minus Glory. She decided to fly home for the weekend and spend some much needed time with her parents. Since it's wet outside from the storm, we are all gathered in the living room. Lisa has even joined in on today's visit and true to her nature has been busy cooking alongside Bella. Once the kids have been fed and put down for naps, we gather in the kitchen again.

"How's the pregnancy going so far, Grace?" Lisa inquiries as I stand with my hand hovering over a large bowl of chips.

"Good so far," I pop a corn chip covered in cheese in my mouth.

"Because of my age, I'm considered high risk, but everything is looking good," I tell her.

"Kids are asleep, so besides the pregnant ladies, who here wants wine?" Alba announces as she enters the kitchen and begins taking glasses down from the cabinet. After pouring one for herself, Lisa, and Emerson, she hands a drink over to Mila.

"Um, I think I'll pass," Mila tells Alba.

"Wait. What?" Bella says. "At dinner the other night, you passed up wine and now again today? You never pass up wine, Mila." Bella eyes her suspiciously. The rest of the ladies have their full attention on Mila, and her eyes dart around the room. She bites her bottom lip for a moment. Caving she explains, "There's a possibility I could be pregnant."

A round of gasps and 'oh my god, that's great' are repeated around the room.

"You haven't taken a test yet?" Emerson immediately questions her.

"No, I'm a week late, though. For some reason, I'm nervous. Reid and I talked about giving it a go about two months ago, but what if it's a false alarm. My heart wants it so much. I don't want to be disappointed."

"Mila, I understand how you feel," Bella looks at her, "We all do," she smiles and rubs her swollen belly. "But I say let's find out. Today." Bella turns and holds her hand out toward her sister. "Come on," she wiggles her fingers, "you carry a pregnancy test around like currency."

Rolling her eyes, Alba crosses the kitchen into the foyer only to return to the kitchen with not one but two different at home pregnancy tests causing all of us to laugh out loud, including herself as she shrugs her shoulders.

Mila briefly excuses herself to the bathroom. Upon returning, she sets the tests carefully on a napkin and onto the counter. Anxiously, we wait for five minutes to pass.

As soon as enough time has passed, Mila walks back to the counter and looks down. Her hand instantly goes to her lower abdomen, and a smile overtakes the nervous look she had on her face. "I'm pregnant."

We surround her with congratulations and hugs. After discussing with Jake just before getting here, I decided to make my announcement on the heels of the new baby news. "Mila, I have something I need to give you before Jake picks me up," I tell her. Retrieving my bag from the kitchen table, I pull out a white envelope and walk back toward my friends, my family. "I came into some money. Money for reasons I'm sure you all would understand I don't want any part of. That being said, I believe it would help others." She opens the envelope containing the check made out to *New Hope House, The Charlotte Scott Foundation.* A halfway home she and Sofia have recently started operating out of her late grandmother's home.

Tears pool in her eyes, "Grace," she whispers. "I was fortunate to find my happily ever after, and I hope this can be a good start at helping others find theirs," I too start to tear up. *Damn hormones.*

Mila doesn't try to give the check back. She doesn't ask questions. She hands the check over to Alba and hugs me and says, "Thank you."

After promising to keep the news of Mila's pregnancy under wraps until she and Reid see a doctor and choose to share it with the rest of the family, we sit around for the next hour laughing and planning another baby shower. Mine.

LATER THAT EVENING, with the house to ourselves, Jake and I spend our time together on the back porch watching the sunset and listening to the soothing sounds of the river's current rush downstream. The weather is turning a little cooler, so Jake goes inside and returns with a blanket large enough to wrap around the both of us. Snuggling as close as I can, I warm myself with the heat of his body. Completely content doing nothing, we sit like this until the darkness of nightfall engulfs us and the stars become our only source of light.

"Look," I point to the sky at a falling star. "Hurry, make a wish," I quickly say as it skirts across the midnight sky.

"Marry me," Jake whispers in my ear.

I turn, connecting my eyes with his. "Is that your wish?" I smile warmly at him.

He pushes my curls from my face and nods. "Marry me, Little Bird."

On a breath, I answer, "Okay."

EPILOGUE

JAKE

"How's my baby girl doing?" I ask Grace, who is currently sittin' on my lap with my hand rubbin' circles on her belly.

"You know it could be a boy," she argues back.

The gender of our baby is somethin' we have been debating back and forth over for weeks. Grace insists the baby is a boy, and I say it's a girl. I don't care either way, but I like messing with my woman. That and my gut says we will have another daughter and usually, my gut feelings are never wrong. Bringing her hand to rest on top of mine, I intertwine our fingers and stare down at our matching gold bands. Grace and I got married today. Once she agreed to be my wife, we didn't waste much time sealing the deal. Neither one of us wanted a big show. When Grace suggested a simple ceremony followed by a party at the clubhouse, that was more proof she was the woman for me. So, with our family and close friends, we stood in front of Quinn, me in my jeans and cut, and Grace in a simple pale-yellow dress with her fiery red curls blowin' in the breeze, as we said I do.

"Are you happy, Little Bird?" I murmur into her ear, causing her skin to prickle.

Nuzzling further into my embrace, she lets out a sigh of contentment. "I'm the happiest I've ever been. I don't know where I'd be if you had given up on me."

"Never gonna happen, babe. Now kiss your husband."

"Look at you, Prez. You're actin' just like them three." Quinn plops his ass down in a chair next to mine and points across from us to where Logan, Gabriel, and Reid are sittin' with their women on their laps.

"Jealous," Reid jabs back.

"Fuck yeah, I'm jealous. I can't wait to be married. It's just takin' a little longer than I expected to seal the deal."

The funny thing is, Quinn is one hundred percent serious. That boy is so hard up for a particular little doctor he can't see straight. The thing about my brother is that he is tenacious. Too bad for him, his goofy behavior gets in his way. People don't tend to take him seriously. Those of us who know Quinn know he means business when he's decided he wants something and knows he will stop at nothing to get it. The question is, how long will his Dr. Pretty hold out? Either way, I have no doubt things between the two will come full circle. Hell, if it can happen for me, Logan, Gabriel, and Reid, then it can happen for anyone. We all have overcome so much. Now Logan and Bella are about to have their baby, Reid fought his demons and found happiness with Mila and her daughter, who happens to be Noah's, and even Gabriel found a woman to put up with his grumpy ass.

For a moment, we all fall silent, and I take a moment to gaze around at my surroundings, and a smile tugs at my lips at the sight of all the children playing. This time next year mine and Grace's child will be out there.

For the most part, everything with The Kings has gone back to normal. Bennett has made a full recovery and is back to doing what he does for the community, and Lisa is back to being herself and fussing over everyone in typical momma bear style.

As for the shop, it should be up and running in about a month or so. Reid and Nikolai, of course, are overseeing the construction. We decided to double the size of the previous building because why the hell not. It was actually Quinn's idea. He suggested that since we were all popping kids out left and right, then why not add a playroom or some shit—his words not mine. Logan had mentioned in the past, Bella missed work but didn't want to give up being a full-time mom. Grace mentioned she would take the baby with her to the bakery a couple days out of the week and then find a sitter for the other days. But when Quinn came up with the idea for the garage, we all jumped on board. This way kid watching duties could be swapped back and forth between the women and us. Nobody has to miss out.

The club is also going to build a playroom at the bakery. Grace said she wanted to make the playroom public and possibly hire someone to look after the children. She said that way, women or men could come in with their children, let them play while they relaxed with their donuts and coffee. When she questioned a few of her customers about the idea, they were quick to say they thought it was a fantastic concept.

"Holy shit!" Logan's voice booms, bringing me out of my thoughts.

"Did you just pee on him?" Quinn asks Bella.

"Seriously, Quinn! No, I did not just pee all over my husband—you ass. My water broke!"

Suddenly Bella is scooped up into Logan's arms, and he's haulin' ass across the yard toward his truck. "I can walk, you know," Bella smarts off, but Logan ignores her and deposits her in the cab of his truck. Meanwhile, the rest of us fly into action hot on their heels. Six hours later, the waiting room of the maternity ward at the hospital is standing room only. Alba has made an appearance every hour to give us updates. On her last update, Bella was fully dilated and ready to push. That was forty-five minutes ago. The double doors open at the end of the hall with a smiling Logan brings us all to our feet.

"Well?" I ask when he steps into the room.

"We have a boy!" he shouts, and the room erupts into chaos. I'm the first to pull him in for a hug. "Congratulations, son."

"Thanks, Jake."

Next, it's Demetri and Nikolai who congratulate him.

"What's his name? How much does he weigh?" Lisa asks.

Looking at both his father and me, Logan announces his son's name. "He weighs 8 lbs 5 oz, and we named him Jake Demetri Kane."

I place my hand on his shoulder, "I'm honored, Logan. Thank you."

"I wouldn't have the life I have if it wasn't for you, Prez. It is me who is honored to name my son after you."

"You know what?" Quinn pipes up after Logan has left to go back to his woman and son. "I'm telling you all right now; I better be the next person to announce they're having a baby."

Emerson, who is sitting across the room chokes on her coffee after Quinn's declaration. I notice Reid shifting from foot to foot while Mila shoots a few strange looks toward Lisa, Emerson, Leah, and Grace. *Oh shit!*

"Actually..." Reid cuts in.

"Oh, hell, no, brother!" Quinn shoots daggers at Reid.

Pulling Mila into his side, Reid continues. "Mila and I are having a baby."

Quinn walks up to Reid and congratulates his brother, and for the second time in less than thirty minutes, the waiting room erupts into cheers.

A FEW MONTHS **later**

"I am beyond ready for this baby to be born," Grace moans as she paces the floor in the living room of our home as she holds her lower back. She's scheduled to have a c-section tomorrow morning because our daughter has not turned to allow for a natural birth.

"Come here. Sit down and let me rub your feet," I pat the couch cushion beside me. Grace shuffles across the wood floor in one of my cotton shirts and a thick pair of wool socks covering her feet. "These aren't feet anymore. They are cankles with toes," she pouts. Slowly, with my help, she lowers her very pregnant body to the sofa and places her tired feet in my lap. "They stay swollen because you refuse to rest. You stay on your feet all day." I begin to rub her swollen feet.

"Oh god, yes," she moans.

"Come on; let's get you to bed," I tell her, trying to suppress a chuckle.

After making it up the stairs, we briefly stop by Remi's room, and Grace knocks on her door. The door swings open. "Mom, are you okay?" she asks with worry.

"Nothing is wrong, Peanut. I'm fine. I only stopped to get a hug. I'll be gone before you wake up in the morning. Glory will bring you to the hospital before they start the surgery." Grace embraces her.

"I can't wait to meet my sister," Remi states.

Pulling away, Grace kisses her forehead, and I lean in doing the same. "Goodnight, sweetheart."

Once in bed with my wife, I rest my hand on her very swollen belly. After several months, tomorrow I get to meet our baby girl.

"You ready for all this? After tonight there will be sleepless nights, dirty diapers, spit up; all these will become our new normal." Grace sighs as she finally adjusts in a position she finds comfort in and settles there for the night.

Our baby girl kicks against my hand. "I've always been ready."

ELLIE KATE DELANE was born two weeks ago at 7:45 am on a beautiful Sunday morning weighing in at 7 lbs and 6 oz. Everything went smooth and according to plan. Our entire family sat in the waiting room on the edge of their seats, and that day I was the one walking through those heavy double doors to announce the birth of my child to all the people in this world who matter the most to me.

It's a big day today. It's Remi's birthday, and this time everyone is out here at our home celebrating with us.

"Can I go for a ride, just down by the river?" Remi begs. Those horses and riding have become everything to her. We even signed her up for riding classes several months back right after things got back to normal. She's a natural born rider. Remi's riding instructor has encouraged her to practice jumping horses so she can enter next year's equestrian show sponsored by the local 4-H club. For her birthday, all she wanted was a new saddle for her horse she calls Spirit, so that's what we bought her. "Sure, just as long as it's okay with your momma, and we can see you from here," I tell her.

She wraps her arms around my waist, hugging me. "I will. Thanks, Dad."

Yes, you heard her right. She calls me dad, and every time she does, my heart melts. On the day her baby sister was born, while she had her turn holding her, Remi started to tear up. The words that followed choked me up so much I lost my shit in front of everyone who was in the room, and that was damn near our entire family. Remi asked if she could call me Dad. She said she wanted to have a daddy like her sister. Remi became mine the moment I found out about her, and there has never been any question in my heart; I was forever going to be her father.

I'm standing outside on the back porch, enjoying a beer with my men as I look in through the window of the kitchen. Grace has just placed our daughter into the arms of her awaiting grandma—my mom, as my pops sits beside them wearing a prideful smile, Pop-Pop to his granddaughters.

"Fuckin' fantastic feeling," Logan stands beside me and remarks as he watches through the window with me.

"Not a better fuckin' feelin' in the world than what I'm feelin' right now, son." I continue to watch my family. Grace turns, catching me watching and smiles brightly. The woman's loving look back at me is the center of my entire existence—my world—my wife—the mother of my children. She doesn't realize she holds so much of my happiness in the palm of her hands.

A higher power granted us a second chance at life. We both found each other—found love when we needed it the most. She would tell you I saved her, but that is far from the truth. Grace saved me. Everything that has ever happened in my life; every person that has touched my life prepared me for this moment in time.

My life is rich, but wealth does not define my worth. I am defined by the people in it who surround me. The beautiful red-haired woman I hold in my arms every night—my Little Bird. My two daughters, whom I love. The men I call my brothers. My family.

I turn and face my boys and raise the beer in my hand. "To Family."

All of them lift their drinks in the air. "To Family."

Lightning Source UK Ltd.
Milton Keynes UK
UKHW021257110722
405684UK00007B/1339